THE CASE OF THE CONSTANT SUICIDES

John Dickson Carr was born in 1906 in Uniontown, Pennsylvania, the son of a lawyer. While at school and college, he wrote ghost, detective and adventure stories. After studying law, he headed to Paris in 1928. Once there, he lost any desire to study law and soon turned to writing crime fiction full-time. His first novel, *It Walks by Night*, was published in 1930. Two years later, he moved to England with his English wife; thereafter he became a prolific author and became a master of the locked-room mystery. He also wrote a biography of Sir Arthur Conan Doyle, radio plays, dozens of short stories, and magazine reviews. He died in 1977 in South Carolina.

The Case of the Constant Suicides

A Gideon Fell Mystery

JOHN DICKSON CARR

Introduced by Robert J. Harris

First published in the United States in 1941 by Harper & Brothers.
This edition published in Great Britain in 2018 by Polygon,
an imprint of Birlinn Ltd.

West Newington House
10 Newington Road
Edinburgh
EH9 1QS

www.polygonbooks.co.uk

1

ISBN 978 1 83697 459 5
eBook ISBN 978 1 78885 052 0

British Library Cataloguing in Publication Data
A catalogue record for this book is available on request
from the British Library.

Typeset by 3btype.com

Printed and bound in Great Britain by Clays Ltd, St Ives plc

John Dickson Carr:
Master of The Impossible

One night in 1945 two non-existent characters sat up into the early hours enthusiastically discussing the intricacies of the 'miracle crime'. These two fictitious persons were Ellery Queen (the joint pen name of cousins Frederic Dannay and Manfred Bennington Lee) and Carter Dickson (a pen name often adopted by John Dickson Carr, which became nearly as famous as his own). We know this conversation took place from the dedication in the 1945 Carter Dickson novel *The Curse of the Bronze Lamp*.

What a pleasure it would have been to eavesdrop on these two giants of the detective genre and hear them explore how a man might walk across the threshold of his own house and disappear into thin air, or be murdered in a locked room that no one else has entered.

John Dickson Carr has long been regarded as the absolute master of the impossible crime, where the question is not merely who is the culprit, but how could this crime possibly have been committed without violating the laws of time and space? How could a man be stabbed to death standing alone on top of a tower?

How could someone be killed by a shot from a gun that is pointed in the opposite direction?

Carr presented his readers with many such puzzles and solved them all ingeniously. But there is far more to the irresistible appeal of John Dickson Carr than mere cleverness. He also excels in delicious Gothic atmosphere, and creates comic scenes worthy of P.G. Wodehouse. In addition to this, as an American who made his home in Britain, he delights in the English countryside and the Scottish Highlands with the freshness and enthusiasm of one who has dreamed of these places long before ever setting eyes on them.

Then there is his cast of wonderful, lively characters, chief among them the magnificent Dr Gideon Fell, the brilliant detective whom you will meet in these pages. Carr based Fell on his literary idol G.K. Chesterton, the essayist and author of the Father Brown stories. He is a Falstaffian figure with a bandit moustache who needs two stout walking sticks to support his impressive bulk. In the first Fell novel (*Hag's Nook*, 1933), an old friend of the good doctor describes him like this: 'The man has more obscure, useless and fascinating information than any person I ever met. He'll ply you with food and whisky until your head reels; he'll talk interminably, on any subject whatsoever, but particularly on the glories and sports of old-time England. He likes band music, melodrama, beer and slapstick comedies; he's a great old boy and you'll like him.'

Indeed, Dr Fell is the one fictional detective in whose company I would love to spend an evening by a roaring fire (with a plentiful supply of beer and cigars, of course). His irrepressible gusto is surely matched by that of his creator, for in the crime genre, Carr's writing is unmatched for its sheer exuberance and the pure joy of storytelling.

And so to *The Case of the Constant Suicides*, which many regard as the most entertaining book he ever wrote. This is quite a compliment when you consider both the quality and the quantity of his output. Here we have a haunted Scottish castle, colourful dashes of comedy and romance, and a series of impossible deaths to be solved. Who could resist it?

We'd best hurry along to Euston station now to catch the night train to Glasgow. At the end of our journey waits a thrilling adventure and the very best of company – Dr Gideon Fell.

Robert J. Harris
St Andrews
2018

Robert J. Harris is the author of *The Thirty-One Kings: Richard Hannay Returns* and the Artie Conan Doyle Mystery series.

1

The 9:15 train for Glasgow pulled out of Euston half an hour late that night, and forty minutes after the sirens had sounded.

When the sirens went, even the dim blue lights along the platform were extinguished.

A milling, jostling, swearing crowd, mainly in khaki, groped about the platform, its shins and knuckles barked by kit and luggage, its hearing deadened by the iron coughing of engines. Lost in it was a youngish professor of history, who was trying to find his sleeping compartment on the Glasgow train.

Not that anyone had cause for apprehension. It was only the first of September, and the heavy raiding of London had not yet begun. We were very young in those days. An air-raid alert meant merely inconvenience, with perhaps one lone raider droning somewhere, and no barrage.

But the professor of history, Alan Campbell (MA, Oxon.; Ph.D, Harvard) bumped along with unacademic profanity. The first-class sleepers appeared to be at the head of a long train. He could see a porter, with much luggage, striking matches at the open door of a carriage, where names were posted on a board opposite the numbers of the compartments assigned to them.

Striking a match in his turn, Alan Campbell discovered that the train appeared to be full and that his own compartment was number four.

He climbed in. Dim little lighted numerals over each door in the corridor showed him the way. When he opened the door of his compartment, he felt distinctly better.

This, he thought, was really first-rate in the way of comfort. The compartment was a tiny metal room, green-painted, with a single berth, nickel washbasin, and a long mirror on the door communicating with the next compartment. Its blackout consisted of a sliding shutter which sealed the window. Though it was intensely hot and close, he saw over the berth a metal ventilator which you could twist to let in air.

Pushing his suitcase under the berth, Alan sat down to get his breath. His reading matter, a Penguin novel and a copy of the *Sunday Watchman*, lay beside him. He eyed the newspaper, and his soul grew dark with bile.

"May he perish in the everlasting bonfire!" Alan said aloud, referring to his only enemy in the world. "May he –"

Then he checked himself, remembering that he ought to remain in a good temper. After all, he had a week's leave; and, though no doubt his mission was sad enough in a formal way, still it was in the nature of a holiday.

Alan Campbell was a Scot who had never in his life set foot in Scotland. For that matter, except for his years at the American Cambridge and a few visits to the Continent, he had never been out of England. He was thirty-five: bookish, serious-minded though not without humor, well-enough looking but perhaps already inclined toward stodginess.

His notions of Scotland were drawn from the novels of Sir Walter Scott or, if he felt in a frivolous mood, John Buchan. Added to this was a vague idea of granite and heather and Scottish jokes – which last he rather resented, showing himself no true Scot in spirit. Now he was at last going to see for himself. And if only –

The sleeping-car attendant knocked at the door, and put his head in.

"Mr Campbell?" he inquired, consulting the little imitation ivory card on the door, on which names could be written with a pencil and rubbed out.

"Dr Campbell," said Alan, not without stateliness. He was still young enough to get a thrill at the newness and unexpectedness of the title.

"What time would you like to be called in the morning, sir?"

"What time do we get to Glasgow?"

"Well, sir, we're *due* in at six-thirty."

"Better call me at six, then."

The attendant coughed. Alan correctly interpreted this.

"Call me half an hour before we do get in, then."

"Yes, sir. Would you like tea and biscuits in the morning?"

"Can I get a proper breakfast on the train?"

"No, sir. Only tea and biscuits."

Alan's heart sank along with his stomach. He had been in such a hurry to pack that he had eaten no dinner, and his inside now felt squeezed up like a concertina. The attendant understood his look.

"If I was you, sir, I should nip out and get something at the buffet now."

"But the train's due to start in less than five minutes!"

"I shouldn't let that worry you, sir. We'll not be starting as soon as that, to my way of thinking."

Yes: he'd better do it.

Ruffled, he left the train. Ruffled, he groped along a noisy and crowded platform in the dark, back through the barrier. When he stood at the buffet, with a slopped cup of tea and some dry sandwiches containing ham cut so thin as to have achieved a degree of transparency, his eye fell again on the *Sunday Watchman*. And bile rose again in his soul.

It has been stated that Alan Campbell had only one enemy in

the world. Indeed, except for a fight in his schooldays in which he had exchanged black eyes and a bloody nose with the boy who later became his best friend, he could not even remember disliking anyone very much.

The man in question was also named Campbell: though he was not, Alan hoped and believed, any relation. The other Campbell lived in a sinister lair at Harpenden, Herts. Alan had never set eyes on him, and did not even know who he was. Yet he disliked him very cordially indeed.

Mr Belloc has pointed out that no controversy can grow more heated, more bitter (or, to a detached observer, more funny) than a controversy between two learned dons over some obscure point that nobody cares twopence about.

We have all, with glee, seen the thing happen. Somebody writes in a dignified newspaper or literary weekly that Hannibal, when crossing the Alps, passed close to the village of Viginum. Some other erudite reader then writes in to say that the name of the village was not Viginum, but Biginium. On the following week, the first writer mildly but acidly deplores your correspondent's ignorance, and begs leave to present the following evidence that it was Viginum. The second writer then says he regrets that an acrimonious note seems to have crept into the discussion, which is no doubt what makes Mr So-and-So forget his manners; but is under the necessity of pointing out –

And that tears it. The row is sometimes good for two or three months.

Something of a similar nature had dropped with a splosh into Alan Campbell's placid life.

Alan, a kindly soul, had meant no offense. He sometimes reviewed historical works for the *Sunday Watchman*, a newspaper very similar to the *Sunday Times* or the *Observer*.

In the middle of June this paper had sent him a book called *The Last Days of Charles the Second*, a weighty study of political events between 1680 and 1685, by K.I. Campbell (MA, Oxon.).

Alan's review of this appeared on the following Sunday, and his sin lay in the following words, toward the end of the notice.

> It cannot be said that Mr Campbell's book throws any fresh light on the subject; and it is not, indeed, free from minor blemishes. Mr Campbell surely cannot believe that Lord William Russell was ignorant of the Rye House Plot. Barbara Villiers, Lady Castlemaine, was created Duchess of Cleveland in 1670: not, as the printer has it, 1680. And what is the reason for Mr Campbell's extraordinary notion that this lady was 'small and auburn-haired'?

Alan sent in his copy on Friday, and forgot the matter. But in the issue nine days later appeared a letter from the author dated at Harpenden, Herts. It concluded:

> May I say that my authority for what your reviewer considers this 'extraordinary' notion is Steinmann, the lady's only biographer. If your reviewer is unfamiliar with this work, I suggest that a visit to the British Museum might repay his trouble.

This riled Alan considerably.

> While I must apologize for drawing attention to so trivial a matter (he wrote), and thank Mr Campbell for his courtesy in drawing my attention to a book with which I am already familiar, nevertheless, I think a visit to the British Museum would be less profitable than a visit to the National Portrait Gallery. There Mr Campbell will find a portrait, by Lely, of this handsome termagant. The hair is shown as jet-black, the proportions as ample. It might be thought that a painter would flatter his subject.

But it cannot be thought that he would turn a blonde into a brunette, or depict any court lady as fatter than she actually was.

That, Alan thought, was rather neat. And not far from devastating either.

But the snake from Harpenden now began to hit below the belt. After a discussion of known portraits, he concluded:

Your reviewer, incidentally, is good enough to refer to this lady as a 'termagant.' What are his reasons for this? They appear to be that she had a temper and that she liked to spend money. When any man exhibits astounded horror over these two qualities in a woman, it is permissible to inquire whether he has ever been married.

This sent Alan clear up in the air. It was not the slur on his historical knowledge that he minded: it was the implication that he knew nothing about women – which, as a matter of fact, was true.

K.I. Campbell, he thought, was in the wrong; and knew it; and was now, as usual, trying to cloud the matter with side-issues. His reply blistered the paper, the more so as the controversy caught on with other readers.

Letters poured in. A major wrote from Cheltenham that his family had for generations been in possession of a painting, said to be that of the Duchess of Cleveland, which showed the hair as medium-brown. A savant from the Athenaeum wanted them to define their terms, saying what proportions they meant by "ample," and in what parts of the body, according to the standards of the present day.

"Bejasus," said the editor of the *Sunday Watchman*, "it's the best thing we've had since Nelson's glass eye. Leave 'em to it."

Throughout July and August the row continued. The

unfortunate mistress of Charles the Second came in for almost as much notoriety as she had known in the days of Samuel Pepys. Her anatomy was discussed in some detail. The controversy was entered, though not clarified, by another savant named Dr Gideon Fell, who seemed to take a malicious delight in confusing the two Campbells, and mixing everybody up.

The editor himself finally called a halt to it. First, because the anatomical detail now verged on the indelicate; and, second, because the parties to the dispute had grown so confused that nobody knew who was calling whom what.

But it left Alan feeling that he would like to boil K.I. Campbell in oil.

For K.I. Campbell appeared every week, dodging like a sharpshooter and always stinging Alan. Alan began to acquire a vague but definite reputation for ungallant conduct, as one who has traduced a dead woman and might traduce any lady of his acquaintance. K.I. Campbell's last letter more than hinted at this.

His fellow members of the faculty joked about it. The undergraduates, he suspected, joked about it. "Rip" was one term; "rounder" another.

He had breathed a prayer of relief when the debate ended. But even now, drinking slopped tea and eating dry sandwiches in a steamy station buffet, Alan stiffened as he turned over the pages of the *Sunday Watchman*. He feared that his eye might light on some reference to the Duchess of Cleveland, and that K.I. Campbell might have sneaked into the columns again.

No. Nothing. Well, at least that was a good omen to start the journey.

The hands of the clock over the buffet stood at twenty minutes to ten.

In sudden agitation Alan remembered his train. Gulping down his tea (when you are in a hurry there always seems to be about a quart of it, boiling hot), he hurried out into the blackout again. For the second time he took some minutes to find his ticket at the barrier, searching through every pocket before he found it in the first one. He wormed through crowds and luggage trucks, spotted the right platform after some difficulty, and arrived back at the door of his carriage just as doors were slamming all along the train, and the whistle blew.

Smoothly gliding, the train moved out.

Off on the great adventure, then. Alan, pleased with life again, stood in the dim corridor and got his breath. Through his mind moved some words out of the letter he had received from Scotland: "The Castle of Shira, at Inveraray, on Loch Fyne." It had a musical, magical sound. He savored it. Then he walked down to his compartment, threw open the door, and stopped short.

An open suitcase, not his own, lay on the berth. It contained female wearing apparel. Bending over it and rummaging in it stood a brown-haired girl of twenty-seven or twenty-eight. She had been almost knocked sprawling by the opening of the door, and she straightened up to stare at him.

"Wow!" said Alan inaudibly.

His first thought was that he must have got the wrong compartment, or the wrong carriage. But a quick glance at the door reassured him. There was his name, Campbell, written in pencil on the imitation-ivory strip.

"I beg your pardon," he said. "But haven't you – er – made a mistake?"

"No, I don't think so," replied the girl, rubbing her arm and staring back at him with increasing coolness.

Even then he noticed how attractive she was, though she wore very little powder or lipstick, and there was a look of determined severity about her rounded face. She was five feet two inches tall, and pleasantly shaped. She had blue eyes, spaced rather wide apart, a good forehead, and full lips which she tried to keep firmly compressed. She wore tweeds, a blue jumper, and tan stockings with flat-heeled shoes.

"But this," he pointed out, "is compartment number four."

"Yes. I know that."

"Madam, what I am trying to indicate is that it's my compartment. My name is Campbell. Here it is on the door."

"And my name," retorted the girl, "happens to be Campbell too. And I must insist that it's *my* compartment. Will you be good enough to leave, please?"

She was pointing to the suitcase.

Alan looked, and looked again. The train rattled and clicked over points, swaying and gathering speed. But what he could not assimilate easily was the meaning of the words painted in tiny white letters on the side of the suitcase.

K.I. Campbell. Harpenden.

2

In Alan's mind and emotions, incredulity was gradually giving way to something very different.

He cleared his throat.

"May I ask," he said sternly, "what the initials 'K.I.' stand for?"

"Kathryn Irene, of course. My first names. But will you *please* –?"

"So!" said Alan. He held up the newspaper. "May I further ask whether you have recently taken part in a disgraceful correspondence in the *Sunday Watchman*?"

Miss K.I. Campbell put up a hand to her forehead as though to shade her eyes. She put the other hand behind her to steady herself on the rim of the wash-basin. The train rattled and jerked. A sudden suspicion, and then comprehension, began to grow in the blue eyes.

"Yes," said Alan. "I am A.D. Campbell, of University College, Highgate."

By his proud and darkly sinister bearing, he might have been saying, "And, Saxon, I am Roderick Dhu." It occurred to him that there was something vaguely ridiculous in his position as he inclined his head sternly, threw the paper on the berth, and folded his arms. But the girl did not take it like this.

"You beast! You weasel! You worm!" she cried passionately.

"Considering, madam, that I have not had the honor of being formally introduced to you, such terms indicate a degree of intimacy which –"

"Nonsense," said K.I. Campbell. "We're second cousins twice removed. But you haven't got a beard!"

Alan instinctively put a hand to his chin.

"Certainly I have not got a beard. Why should you suppose that I had a beard?"

"We all thought you had. We all thought you had a beard this long," cried the girl, putting her hand at about the level of her waist. "And big double-lensed spectacles. And a nasty, dry, sneering way of talking. You've got that, though. On top of which, you come bursting in here and knock me about –"

Belatedly, she began to rub her arm again.

"Of all the nasty, sneering, *patronizing* book reviews that were ever written," she went on, "that one of yours –"

"There, madam, you show a want of understanding. It was my duty, as a professional historian, to point out certain errors, glaring errors –"

"Errors!" said the girl. "Glaring errors, eh?"

"Exactly. I do not refer to the trivial and meaningless point about the Duchess of Cleveland's hair. I refer to matters of real moment. Your treatment of the elections of 1680, if you will excuse my plain speaking, would make a cat laugh. Your treatment of Lord William Russell was downright dishonest. I do not say that he was as big a crook as your hero Shaftesbury. Russell was merely a muttonhead: 'of,' as it was put at the trial, 'imperfect understanding'; to be pitied, if you like, but not to be pictured as anything except the traitor he was."

"You're nothing," said K.I. Campbell furiously, "but a beastly *Tory!*"

"In reply, I quote no less an authority than Dr Johnson. 'Madam, I perceive that you are a vile Whig.'"

Then they stood and looked at each other.

Alan didn't ordinarily talk like this, you understand. But he was so mad and so much on his dignity that he could have given points and a beating to Edmund Burke.

"Who are you, anyway?" he asked in a more normal tone, after a pause.

This had the effect of putting Kathryn Campbell again on her dignity. She compressed her lips. She drew herself up to the full majesty of five feet two.

"Though I consider myself under no obligation to answer that question," she replied, putting on a pair of shell-rimmed glasses which only increased her prettiness, "I don't mind telling you that I am a member of the department of history at the Harpenden College for Women –"

"Oh."

"Yes. And as capable as any man, more so, of dealing with the period in question. Now will you *please* have the elementary decency to get out of my compartment?"

"No, I'm damned if I do! It's not your compartment!"

"I say it is my compartment."

"And I say it's not your compartment."

"If you don't get out of here, *Dr* Campbell, I'll ring the bell for the attendant."

"Please do. If you don't, I'll ring it myself."

The attendant, brought running by two peals on the bell each made by a different hand, found two stately but almost gibbering professors attempting to tell their stories.

"I'm sorry, ma'am," said the attendant, worriedly consulting his list, "I'm sorry, sir; but there seems to have been a mistake somewhere. There's only one Campbell down here, without even a 'Miss' or a 'Mr'. I don't know what to say."

Alan drew himself up.

"Never mind. Not for the world," he declared loftily, "would I disturb this lady in possession of her ill-gotten bed. Take me to another compartment."

Kathryn gritted her teeth.

"No, you don't, *Dr* Campbell. I am not accepting any favors on the grounds of my sex, thank you. Take *me* to another compartment."

The attendant spread out his hands.

"I'm sorry, miss. I'm sorry, sir. But I can't do that. There's not a sleeper to be had on the whole train. Not a seat either, if it comes to that. They're even standing in third class."

"Never mind," snapped Alan, after a slight pause. "Just let me get my bag from under there, and I'll stand up in the corridor all night."

"Oh, don't be silly," said the girl in a different voice. "You can't do that."

"I repeat, madam –"

"All the way to Glasgow? You can't do that. Don't be silly!"

She sat down on the edge of the berth.

"There's only one thing we can possibly do," she added. "We'll share this compartment, and sit up all night."

A powerful shade of relief went over the attendant.

"Now, miss, that's very kind of you! And I know this gentleman appreciates it. Don't you, sir? If you wouldn't mind, I'm sure the company'll make it right with you at the other end. It's very kind of the lady, isn't it, sir?"

"No, it is not. I refuse –"

"What's the matter, Dr Campbell?" asked Kathryn, with icy sweetness. "Are you afraid of me? Or is it that you just daren't face historical fact when it is presented to you?"

Alan turned to the attendant. Had there been room, he would have pointed to the door with a gesture as dramatic as that of a father turning out his child into the storm in an old-fashioned melodrama. As it was, he merely banged his hand on the ventilator. But the attendant understood.

"Then that's all right, sir. Good night." He smiled. "It shouldn't be so unpleasant, should it?"

"What do you mean by that?" Kathryn demanded sharply.

"Nothing, miss. Good night. Sleep – I mean, good night."

Again they stood and looked at each other. They sat down, with mutual suddenness, at opposite ends of the berth. Though they had been fluent enough before, now that the door was closed they were both covered with pouring self-consciousness.

The train was moving slowly: steadily, yet with a suggestion of a jerk, which probably meant a raider somewhere overhead. It was less hot now that air gushed down the ventilator.

It was Kathryn who broke the tension of self-consciousness. Her expression began as a superior smile, turned into a giggle, and presently dissolved in helpless laughter. Presently Alan joined in.

"Sh-h!" she urged in a whisper. "We'll disturb the person in the next compartment. But we have been rather ridiculous, haven't we?"

"I deny that. At the same time –"

Kathryn removed her spectacles and wrinkled up her smooth forehead.

"Why are you going north, Dr Campbell? Or should I say Cousin Alan?"

"For the same reason, I suppose, that you are. I got a letter from a man named Duncan, who bears the impressive title of Writer to the Signet."

"In Scotland," said Kathryn, with a cutting condescension, "a Writer to the Signet is a lawyer. Really, Dr Campbell! Such ignorance! Haven't you ever been in Scotland?"

"No. Have you?"

"Well – not since I was a little girl. But I do take the trouble to keep myself informed, especially about my own flesh and blood. Did the letter say anything else?"

"Only that old Angus Campbell had died a week ago; that such few members of the family as could be found were being informed; and could I find it convenient to come up to the Castle

of Shira, at Inveraray, for a family conference? He made it clear
that there was no question of inheritance, but not quite so clear
what he meant by 'family conference.' *I* used it as a good excuse
to get leave for a much-needed holiday."

Kathryn sniffed. "Really, Dr Campbell! Your own flesh and
blood!"

And Alan found his exasperation rising again.

"Oh, look here! I'd never even heard of Angus Campbell.
I looked him up, through a very complicated genealogy, and
found that he's a cousin of my father. But I never knew him, or
anybody near him. Did you?"

"Well . . ."

"In fact, I'd never even heard of the Castle of Shira. How do
we get there, by the way?"

"At Glasgow, you take a train to Gourock. At Gourock you
get a boat across to Dunoon. At Dunoon you hire a car and drive
out round Loch Fyne to Inveraray. You used to be able to go from
Dunoon to Inveraray by water, but they've stopped that part of
the steamer service since the war."

"And what is that in? The Highlands or the Lowlands?"

This time Kathryn's glance was withering.

Alan would not pursue the matter further. He had a hazy
idea that in estimating the Lowlands or the Highlands, you just
drew a line across the map of Scotland about the middle; that
the upper part would be the Highlands, the lower part the
Lowlands; and there you were. But now he felt somehow that it
could not be quite as simple as this.

"Really, Dr Campbell! It's in the Western Highlands, of course."

"This Castle of Shira," he pursued, allowing (though with
reluctance) his imagination some play. "It's a moated-grange sort
of place, I suppose?"

"In Scotland," said Kathryn, "a castle can be almost anything.
No: it's not a big place like the Duke of Argyll's castle. Or at least
I shouldn't think so from photographs. It stands at the entrance to

Glen Shira, a little way off from Inveraray by the edge of the loch. It's rather a slatternly-looking stone building with a high tower. "But it's got a history. You, as a historian, of course wouldn't know anything about that. That's what makes it all so interesting: the way Angus Campbell died."

"So? How did he die?"

"He committed suicide," returned Kathryn calmly. "Or he was murdered."

The Penguin novel which Alan had brought along was bound in green for a crime thriller. He did not read such things often, but he considered it his duty, sometimes, in the way of relaxation. He stared from this back to Kathryn's face.

"He was – *what?*" Alan almost yelped.

"Murdered. Of course you hadn't heard about that either? Dear me! Angus Campbell jumped or was thrown from a window at the top of the tower."

Alan searched his wits.

"But wasn't there an inquest?"

"They don't have inquests in Scotland. In the event of a suspicious death, they have what is called a 'public inquiry,' under the direction of a man named the Procurator Fiscal. But if they think it's murder, they don't hold the public inquiry at all. That's why I've been watching the *Glasgow Herald* all week, and there's been no report of an inquiry. It doesn't necessarily mean anything, of course."

The compartment was almost cool. Alan reached out and twisted the mouth of the ventilator, which was hissing beside his ear. He fished in his pocket.

"Cigarette?" he offered, producing a packet.

"Thanks. I didn't know you smoked. I thought you used snuff."

"And why," said Alan with austerity, "should you imagine that I used snuff?"

"It got into your beard," explained Kathryn, making motions

of intense disgust. "And dropped all over everywhere. It was horrid. Big-breasted hussy, anyway!"

"Big-breasted hussy? Who?"

"The Duchess of Cleveland."

He blinked at her. "But I understood, Miss Campbell, that you were the lady's particular champion. For nearly two and a half months you've been vilifying my character because you said I vilified hers."

"Oh, well. You seemed to have a down on her. So I had to take the other side, hadn't I?"

He stared at her.

"And this," he said, whacking his knee, "*this* is intellectual honesty!"

"Do you call it intellectual honesty when you deliberately sneered at and patronized a book because you knew it had been written by a woman?"

"But I didn't know it had been written by a woman. I specifically referred to you as 'Mr Campbell,' and –"

"That was only to throw people off the track."

"See here," pursued Alan, lighting her cigarette with a somewhat shaky hand, and lighting his own. "Let us get this straight. I have no down on women scholars. Some of the finest scholars I've ever known have been women."

"Listen to the patronizing way he says *that!*"

"The point is, Miss Campbell, that it would have made no difference to my notice whether the writer of the book had been a man or a woman. Errors are errors, whoever writes them."

"Indeed?"

"Yes. And for the sake of truth will you now admit to me, strictly in private and between ourselves, that you were all wrong about the Duchess of Cleveland being small and auburn-haired?"

"I most certainly will not!" cried Kathryn, putting on her spectacles again and setting her face into its severest lines.

"Listen!" he said desperately. "Consider the evidence! Let me quote to you an example, an instance I could hardly have used in the newspaper. I refer to Pepys's story –"

Kathryn looked shocked.

"Oh, come, Dr Campbell! You, who pretend to be a serious historian, actually give any credit to a story which Pepys received at third hand from his hairdresser?"

"No, no, no, madam. You persist in missing the point. The point is not whether the story is true or apocryphal. The point is that Pepys, who saw the lady so often, could have believed it. Very well! He writes that Charles the Second and the Duchess of Cleveland (who was then Lady Castlemaine) weighed each other; 'and she, being with child, was the heavier.' When we remember that Charles, though lean, was six feet tall and on the muscular side, this makes out the lady to be rather a fine figure of a woman.

"Then there is the account of her mock marriage with Frances Stewart, in which she acted the part of the bridegroom. Frances Stewart was herself no flyweight. But is it reasonable to suppose that the part of the bridegroom was enacted by the smaller and lighter woman?"

"Pure inference."

"An inference, I submit, warranted by the facts. Next we have Reresby's statement –"

"Steinmann says –"

"Reresby makes quite clear –"

"*Hey!*" interrupted an exasperated voice from the next compartment, followed by a rapping on the metal door. "*Oi!*"

Both disputants instantly piped down. For a long time there was a guilty silence, broken only by the flying click and rattle of the wheels.

"Let's turn out the light," whispered Kathryn, "and draw the blackout, and see what's going on outside."

"Right."

The click of the light-switch appeared to satisfy the disturbed occupant of the next compartment.

Pushing aside Kathryn's suitcase in the dark, Alan pulled back the sliding metal shutter from the window.

They were rushing through a dead world, pitch-black except where, along a purple horizon, moved a maze of searchlights. Jack's beanstalk went no higher than these white beams. The white lines shuttled back and forth, in unison, like dancers. They heard no noise except the click of the wheels: not even the waspish, coughing drone of *war-war, war-war*, which marks the cruising bomber.

"Do you think he's following the train?"

"I don't know."

A sense of intimacy, uneasy and yet exhilarating, went through Alan Campbell. They were both crowded close to the window. The two cigarette-ends made glowing red cores, reflected in the glass, pulsing and dimming. He could dimly see Kathryn's face.

The same powerful self-consciousness suddenly overcame them again. They both spoke at the same time, in a whisper.

"The Duchess of Cleveland —"

"Lord William Russell —"

The train sped on.

3

At three o'clock on the following afternoon, a mellow day of Scotland's most golden weather, Kathryn and Alan Campbell were walking up the hill comprising the one main street in Dunoon, Argyllshire.

The train, due to reach Glasgow at half past six in the morning, actually got there toward one o'clock in the afternoon. By this time they were ravenously, ragingly hungry, but still they got no lunch.

An amiable porter, whose conversation was all but unintelligible to both Campbells, informed them that the train for Gourock left in five minutes. So they piled into this, and were borne lunchless along Clydeside to the coast.

To Alan Campbell it had been a considerable shock when he woke in the morning, tousled and unshaven, to find himself hunched back against the cushions of a railway carriage, and a good-looking girl asleep with her head on his shoulder.

But, once he had collected his scattered wits, he decided that he loved it. A sense of adventure was winging straight into his stodgy soul, and making him drunk. There is nothing like spending the night with a girl, even platonically, to remove a sense of constraint. Alan was surprised and somewhat disappointed, on king out of the window, to see that the scenery was still the ame as it was in England: no granite cliffs or heather yet. For he wanted an excuse to quote Burns.

They washed and dressed, these two roaring innocents, to the accompaniment of a stern debate – carried on through a closed door and above the splash of running water – about the Earl of Danby's financial reconstruction policy of 1679. They concealed their hunger well, even in the train to Gourock. But when they discovered, aboard the squat tan-funneled steamer which carried them across the bay to Dunoon, that there was food to be had below, they pitched into Scotch broth and roast lamb with silence and voracity.

Dunoon, white and gray and dun-roofed, lay along the steel-gray water in the shelter of low-lying purple hills. It looked like a good version of all the bad paintings of Scottish scenery which hang in so many houses: except that these usually include a stag, and this did not.

"I now understand," Alan declared, "why there are so many of these daubs. The bad painter cannot resist Scotland. It gives him the opportunity to smear in his purples and yellows, and contrast 'em with water."

Kathryn said that this was nonsense. She also said, as the steamer churned in and butted the pier sideways, that if he did not stop whistling "Loch Lomond" she would go crazy.

Leaving their suitcases at the pier, they crossed the road to a deserted tourist agency and arranged for a car to take them to Shira.

"Shira, eh?" observed the dispirited-looking clerk, who talked like an Englishman. "Getting to be quite a popular place." He gave them a queer look which Alan was afterwards to remember. "There's another party going to Shira this afternoon. If you wouldn't mind sharing the car, it 'ud come less expensive."

"Hang the expense," said Alan, his first words in Dunoon; and it is merely to be recorded that the advertising posters did not drop off the wall. "Still, we don't want to seem uppish. It's another Campbell, I imagine?"

"No," said the clerk, consulting a pad, "this gentleman's name is Swan. Charles E. Swan. He was in here not five minutes ago."

"Never heard of him." Alan looked at Kathryn. "That's not the heir to the estate, by any chance?"

"Nonsense!" said Kathryn. "The heir is Dr Colin Campbell, Angus's first brother."

The clerk looked still more odd. "Yes. We drove him out there yesterday. Very positive sort of gentleman. Well, sir, will you share Mr Swan's car, or have one of your own?"

Kathryn intervened. "We'll share Mr Swan's car, of course, if he doesn't mind. The idea! Flinging good money about like that! When will it be ready?"

"Half past three. Come back here in about half an hour, and you'll find it waiting. Good day, ma'am. Good day, sir. Thank you."

They wandered out into the mellow sunshine, happily, and up the main street looking into shop windows. These appeared to be mainly souvenir shops, and everywhere the eye was dazzled by the display of tartans. There were tartan ties, tartan mufflers, tartan-bound books, tartan-painted tea sets, tartans on the dolls and tartans on the ashtrays – usually the Royal Stewart, as being the brightest.

Alan began to be afflicted with that passion for buying things which overcomes the stoutest traveler. In this he was discouraged by Kathryn, until they reached a haberdasher's some distance up on the right, which displayed in its windows tartan shields (Campbell of Argyll, Macleod, Gordon, Macintosh, MacQueen) which you hung on the wall. These conquered even Kathryn.

"They're lovely," she admitted. "Let's go in."

The shop bell pinged, but went unheard in the argument which was going on at the counter. Behind the counter stood a stern-looking little woman with her hands folded. In front of the counter stood a tallish, leather-faced young man in his late thirties, with a soft hat pushed back on his forehead. He was surrounded by a huge assortment of tartan neckties.

"They're very nice," he was saying courteously. "But they're not what I want. I want to see a necktie with the tartan of the Clan MacHolster. Don't you understand? MacHolster. M-a-c, H-o-l-s-t-e-r, MacHolster. Can't you show me the tartan of the Clan MacHolster?"

"There isna any Clan MacHolster," said the proprietress.

"Now look," said the young man, leaning one elbow on the counter and holding up a lean forefinger in her face. "I'm a Canadian; but I've got Scottish blood in my veins and I'm proud of it. Ever since I was a kid, my father's said to me, 'Charley, if you ever go to Scotland, if you ever get to Argyllshire, you look up the Clan MacHolster. We're descended from the Clan MacHolster, as I've heard your grandad say many a time.'"

"I keep telling ye: there isna any Clan MacHolster."

"But there's *got* to be a Clan MacHolster!" pleaded the young man, stretching out his hands. "There could be a Clan MacHolster, couldn't there? With all the clans and people in Scotland? There *could* be a Clan MacHolster?"

"There could be a Clan MacHitler. But there isna."

His bewildered dejection was so evident that the proprietress took pity on him.

"What wad your name be, now?"

"Swan. Charles E. Swan."

The proprietress cast up her eyes and reflected.

"Swan. That'd be the MacQueens."

Mr Swan seized eagerly at this. "You mean I'm related to the clan of the MacQueens?"

"I dinna ken. Ye may be. Ye may not be. Some Swans are."

"Have you got their tartan here?"

The proprietress showed it to him in a necktie. It was undoubtedly striking, its predominating color being a rich scarlet, and took Mr Swan's fancy at once.

24

"Now that's what I call something like it!" he announced fervently, and turned round and appealed to Alan. "Don't you think so, sir?"

"Admirable. Bit on the loud side for a necktie, though, isn't it?"

"Yes, I like it myself," agreed Mr Swan musingly, holding the tie at arm's length like a painter studying perspective. "Yes. This is the tie for me. I'll take a dozen of 'em."

The proprietress reeled.

"A *dozen*?"

"Sure. Why not?"

The proprietress felt compelled to sound a note of warning. "They're three-and-saxpence each."

"That's all right. Wrap 'em up. I'll take 'em."

As the proprietress bustled off through a door at the back of the shop, Swan turned round with a confidential air. He removed his hat out of deference to Kathryn, revealing a mop of wiry mahogany-colored hair.

"You know," he confided in a low voice, "I've traveled a lot in my time; but this is the queerest damn country *I* ever got into."

"Yes?"

"Yes. All they seem to do is run around telling each other Scotch jokes. I dropped into the bar of the hotel down there, and the local comedian was bringing the house down with nothing but Scotch jokes. And there's another thing. I've only been in this country a few hours – got in by the London train this morning – but on four different occasions I've been buttonholed with the same joke."

"We haven't had that experience so far."

"But *I* have. They hear me talk, see? Then they say, 'You're an American, eh?' I say, 'No, Canadian.' But that doesn't stop 'em. They say, 'Have you heard about my brother Angus, who wouldn't even give the bloodhounds a scent?'"

He paused expectantly.

The faces of his listeners remained impassive.

"Don't you get it?" demanded Swan. "Wouldn't even give the bloodhounds a cent. C-e-n-t, s-c-e-n-t."

"The point of the story," replied Kathryn, "is fairly obvious; but –"

"Oh, I didn't say it *was funny*," Swan hastened to assure them. "I'm just telling you how queer it sounds. You don't find mothers-in-law running around telling each other the latest mother-in-law jokes. You don't find the English telling each other stories about the Englishman getting the point of the joke wrong."

"Are the English," inquired Alan with interest, "popularly supposed to do that?"

Swan flushed a little.

"Well, they are in the stories told in Canada and the States. No offense. You know the kind of thing. 'You cannot drive a nail with a sponge no matter how hard you soak it,' rendered as, 'You cannot drive a nail with a sponge no matter how wet it is.' Now, wait! I didn't say *that* was funny either. I only –"

"Never mind," said Alan. "What I really wanted to ask: are you the Mr Swan who's hired a car to go out to Shira this afternoon?"

A curiously evasive look went over Swan's leathery face, with the fine wrinkles round eyes and mouth. He seemed on the defensive.

"Yes. That's right. Why?"

"We're going out there ourselves, and we were wondering whether you'd mind if we shared the car. My name is Campbell, Dr Campbell. This is my cousin, Miss Kathryn Campbell."

Swan acknowledged the introductions with a bow. His expression changed, and lit up with good nature.

"Not the least little bit in the world! Only too pleased to have you!" he declared heartily. His light gray eyes quickened and shifted. "Members of the family, eh?"

"Distant ones. And you?"

The evasive look returned.

"Well, since you know what my name is, and that I'm related to the MacHolsters or the MacQueens, I couldn't very well pretend to be a member of the family, could I? Tell me, though." He grew more confidential. "What can you tell me about a Miss or Mrs Elspat Campbell?"

Alan shook his head, but Kathryn came to the rescue.

"Aunt Elspat, you mean?"

"I'm afraid I don't know anything about her, Miss Campbell."

"Aunt Elspat," replied Kathryn, "isn't really an aunt, and her name isn't Campbell, though they all call her that. Nobody quite knows who she is or where she came from. She just walked in one day, forty years or so ago, and she's been there ever since. Sort of female head of Shira. She must be nearly ninety, and she's supposed to be rather a terror. I've never met her, though."

"Oh," said Swan, but volunteered no more. The proprietress brought him his parcel of neckties, and he paid for it.

"Which reminds me," he went on, "that we'd better get going, if we want to be in time for that car."

After bidding an elaborate farewell to the proprietress, Swan held open the shop door for them.

"It must be a good way out there, and I want to get back before dark; I'm not staying. I suppose they have the blackout up here too? I want a decent night's rest tonight for once. I sure didn't get one on the train last night."

"Can't you sleep on trains?"

"It wasn't that. There was a married couple in the next compartment, having a hell of a row about some dame from Cleveland, and I hardly closed my eyes all night."

Alan and Kathryn cast a quick, uneasy glance at each other, but Swan was preoccupied with his grievance.

"I've lived in Ohio myself; know it well; that's why I listened. But I couldn't get this thing straight. There was some guy named Russell, and another one called Charles. But whether the dame from Cleveland was running around with Russell, or with Charles, or with this woman's husband, I never did make out. You just heard enough so that you couldn't understand anything. I knocked on the wall, but even after they'd turned out the light –"

"Dr Campbell!" cried Kathryn warningly.

But the murder was out.

"I'm afraid," said Alan, "that that must have been us."

"You?" said Swan. He stopped short in the hot, bright, drowsy street. His eyes traveled to Kathryn's ringless left hand. They seemed to be registering something, as though writing it down.

Then he continued, with such a jerking and obvious change of subject that even his smooth voice added to the obviousness of it.

"They certainly don't seem to be feeling any shortage of food up here, anyway. Look at these grocery-store windows! That stuff over there is haggis. It –"

Kathryn's face was scarlet.

"Mr Swan," she said curtly, "may I assure you that you are making a mistake? I am a member of the Department of History at the Harpenden College for Women –"

"It's the first time I ever saw haggis, but I can't say I like the look of it. It can manage to look nakeder than any meat I ever did see. That stuff that looks like slices of baloney is called Ulster fry. It –"

"Mr Swan, will you *please* give me your attention? This gentleman is Dr Campbell, of University College, Highgate. We can both assure you –"

Again Swan stopped short. He peered round as though to make sure they were not overheard, and then spoke in a low, rapid, earnest voice.

"Look, Miss Campbell," he said, "I'm broadminded. I know how these things are. And I'm sorry I ever brought the subject up."

"But –!"

"All that business about my losing sleep was a lot of bunk. I went to sleep just as soon as you turned the light out, and didn't hear a thing afterwards. So let's just forget I ever spoke about it, shall we?"

"Perhaps that would be best," agreed Alan.

"Alan Campbell, do you *dare* . . ."

Swan, his manner soothing, pointed ahead. A comfortable blue five-seater car was drawn up before the tourist office, with a chauffeur in cap, uniform, and leggings, leaning against it.

"There's the golden chariot," Swan added. "And I've got a guide-book. Come on. Let's enjoy ourselves."

4

Past the tiny shipyard, past the Holy Loch, under heavy timber-furred hills, up the rise past Heather Jock, and into the long, straight stretch beside deep Loch Eck, the car sped on.

They took to the driver at once.

He was a burly, red-faced, garrulous man with a singularly bright blue eye and a vast fund of secret inner amusement. Swan sat in front with him, while Alan and Kathryn sat in the rear. Swan began by being fascinated with the driver's accent, and ended by trying to imitate it.

Pointing to a trickle of water down the hillside, the driver said that this was a "wee burn." Swan seized on the words as a good thing. Henceforward water in any form, even a mountain torrent which would have carried away a house, became a wee burn: Swan calling attention to it and experimentally giving the letter "r" a sound like a death rattle or a singularly sustained gargle.

He did this to Alan's intense discomfort, but Alan need not have minded. The driver did not mind. It was as though (say) Sir Cedric Hardwicke were to hear the purity of his English commented on with amusement by Mr Schnozzle Durante.

Those who regarded Scotsmen as dour or uncommunicative, Alan thought, should have listened to this one. It was impossible to stop him talking. He gave details of every place they passed; and, surprisingly, as it turned out from Swan's guidebook later, with accuracy.

His usual work, he said, was driving a hearse. He entertained them with a description of the many fine funerals, to which he referred with modest pride, where he had had the honor of conducting the corpse. And this gave Swan an opportunity.

"You didn't happen to drive the hearse at a funeral about a week ago, did you?"

To their left, Loch Eck lay like an old tarnished mirror among the hills. No splash or ripple stirred it. Nothing moved on the slopes of fir and pine, stretching up to a pate of outcropping rock, which closed it in. What deadened the mind was the quality of utter silence here, of barriers against the world, and yet of awareness behind it: as though these hills still hid the shaggy shields.

The driver was silent for so long a time, his big red hands gripped round the wheel, that they thought he could not have heard or understood. Then he spoke.

"That'd be auld Campbell of Shira," he stated.

"Aye," said Swan, with perfect seriousness. The thing was infectious: Alan had several times been on the point of saying this himself.

"And ye'll be Campbells tu, I'm thinkin'?"

"Those two are," said Swan, jerking his head toward the two in the rear. "I'm a MacHolster, sometimes called MacQueen."

The driver turned round and looked very hard at him. But Swan was perfectly sincere.

"I drove one of 'em yesterday," said the driver grudgingly. "Colin Campbell it was; and as guid a Scot as masel', for a' he talked like an Englishman."

His face darkened.

"Such bletherin' and blusterin' ye niver heard! An atheist forbye, and thocht nae shame tae admit it! Cau'd me ivery name he caud lay his tongue tu," glowered the driver, "for sayin' Shira is no' a canny place. And it isna either."

Again there was a heavy silence, while the tires sang.

"Canny, I suppose," observed Alan, "being the opposite of uncanny?"

"Aye."

"But if Shira isn't a canny place, what's wrong with it? Ghosts?"

The driver whacked the steering-wheel with a slow and dogged hand, as though he were setting a stamp on it.

"I'm no' sayin' it's ghaists, I'm no' sayin' *wha'* it is. I'm sayin' it isna a canny place, and it isna."

Swan, after whistling between his teeth, opened the guide-book. While the car jolted, and the long afternoon light grew less golden, he turned to the section devoted to Inverarary. He read aloud:

"Before entering the town by the main road, the traveler should look (left) at the *Castle of Shira.*

This building contains no features of architectural interest. It was built toward the end of the sixteenth century, but has since been added to. It will be recognized by its round tower, with a conical slate roof, at the south-eastern corner. This tower, sixty-two feet high, is thought to have been the first effort in an ambitious scheme of building which was later abandoned.

Tradition has it that in 1692, following the massacre of Glencoe in February of that year –"

Swan interrupted himself.

"Hold on!" he said, rubbing his jaw. "I've heard about the massacre of Glencoe. I remember, when I was at school in Detroit . . . What the devil's the matter with *him?* Hoy!"

The driver, his good-humor now restored, was bending back and forth over the wheel in paroxysms of silent inner amusement, so that tears stood in his eyes.

"What is it, governor?" demanded Swan. "What's wrong?"

The driver choked. His inner mirth seemed like torture.

"I *thocht* ye were an American," he declared. "Tell me, noo. Hae ye heard aboot ma brither Angus, who wadna e'en gie the bluid-hoonds a scent?"

Swan smote his forehead.

"Man, dinna ye see it? Hae ye no sense o' humor? C-e-n-t, cent; s-c-e-n-t, scent."

"Curiously enough," said Swan, "I do see it. And I'm not an American; I'm a Canadian, even if I did go to school in Detroit. If anybody Brother-Anguses me again today, I'll slaughter him. Which reminds me. (Stop chortling, can't you? Preserve a proper Scottish gravity!)

"But about this massacre of Glencoe. We acted it out in a play at school long ago. Somebody massacred somebody. What I can't remember is whether the MacDonalds killed the Campbells, or the Campbells killed the MacDonalds."

It was Kathryn who answered him.

"The Campbells killed the MacDonalds, of course," she returned. "I say: they're not still touchy about it in these parts, are they?"

The driver, wiping the tears out of his eyes and becoming stern again, assured her that they weren't.

Swan opened the book again.

"Tradition has it that in 1692, following the massacre of Glencoe in February of that year, Ian Campbell, a soldier in the troop of Campbell of Glenlyon, was so embittered by remorse that he committed suicide by leaping from the topmost window of the tower, dashing out his brains on the paving stones below."

Swan looked up.

"That isn't what happened to the old man the other day?"
"Aye."

"Another tradition is that this suicide was not caused by remorse, but by the 'presence' of one of his victims, whose mangled body pursued him from room to room, until he had no alternative to keep it from touching him except to —"

Swan shut up the book with a snap. "I think that's enough," he added. His eyes narrowed, and his voice grew soft. "What happened, by the way? The old man didn't sleep up at the top of the tower, did he?"

But the driver was not to be drawn. Ask no questions, his bearing intimated, and you will be told no lies.

"Ye'll be sein' Loch Fyne i' a moment, and then Shira," he said. "Ah! Luke, now!"

Reaching a crossroads, they turned to the right at Strachar. A glimmer of water spread out before them. And not a person there but uttered an exclamation of sheer appreciation.

The loch seemed long, wide, and southwards, to their left, endless. Southwards it curved in sun-silvered widening, between heavy banks, for miles to join the Firth of Clyde.

But northwards it lay landlocked – narrower, timelessly placid, its glimmering water slate-colored – and ran in the shape of a wedge to its end some three miles away. The smooth-molded hills, black or dark purple except where stray sunlight caught a splashing of pale purple heather or the dark green of pine and fir, closed round it as though patted into shape with a tone of underlying brown.

Far across the loch, along the water's edge, they could dimly see the low-lying white houses of a town, partly screened behind a belt of trees. They saw a church steeple; and, on the dominating hill above, a dot that looked like a watch-tower. So clear was the air that even at this distance Alan could have sworn he saw the white houses mirrored in the motionless water.

The driver pointed.

"Inveraray," he said.

Their car swept on. Swan was evidently so fascinated that he even forgot to point out wee burns.

The road – a very good one, like all the roads they had seen so far – ran straight along the bank of the loch parallel with its length towards the north. Thus to reach Inveraray, which was on the opposite bank, they would have to drive to the head of the loch, circle round it, and come back on a parallel course to a point opposite where they were now.

This, at least, was what Alan thought. Inveraray looked very close now, just across the gleaming water at its narrowest. Alan was leaning back expansively, taking comfort from the vast, strong hills, when the car stopped with a jerk and the driver climbed out.

"Ge' out," he beamed. "Donald MacLeish'll have a boat here, I'm thinkin'."

They stared at him.

"Did you say boat?" exploded Swan.

"Aye."

"But what in Satan's name do you want a boat for?"

"Tae row ye across."

"But the road goes there, doesn't it? Can't you just drive 'way up there, and come round into Inveraray on the other side?"

"Waste petrol when I've got ma arms?" demanded the driver, not without horror. "No si' a fule! Ge' out. It's five, sax miles by the road."

"Well," smiled Kathryn, who seemed to be preserving her gravity only with considerable effort, "I'm sure *I* don't mind a turn on the water."

"Nor me," conceded Swan, "provided somebody else does the rowing. But, my God, man!" He searched the air with gestures.

"What's the big idea? It's not your petrol, is it? It belongs to the company, doesn't it?"

"Aye. But the preenciple's the same. Ge' in."

An almost extravagantly solemn trio, with the driver very cheerful at the oars, was ferried across the loch in the hush of early evening.

Kathryn and Alan, their suitcases at their feet, sat in the stern of the boat facing toward Inverarary. It was that hour when the water seems lighter and more luminous than the sky, and there are shadows.

"Brr!" said Kathryn presently.

"Cold?"

"A little. But it's not that." She looked at the driver, now the ferryman. "That's the place, isn't it? Over there, where there's a little landing-stage?"

"That's it," agreed the other, craning round to peer over his shoulder. The rowlocks creaked painfully. "It isna much tae luke at; but they do say, mind, that auld Angus Campbell left mair siller than ye caud shake a stick at."

Silently they watched the Castle of Shira grow up and out at them.

It was some distance away from the town, and faced the loch. Built of ancient stone and brick painted gray, with a steep-pitched slate roof, it straggled along the water-side; Kathryn's word, "slatternly", occurred to Alan in connection with it.

Most of all you noticed the tower. Round, and of moss-patched gray stone, it reared up to a conical slate roof at the south-eastern angle of the house. On the side facing the loch it appeared to have only one window. This was a latticed window, with two lights, set close up near the roof; and from there to the uneven flagstones which paved the ground in front of the house must have been close to sixty feet.

Alan thought of the sickening plunge from that window, and moved uneasily.

"I suppose," Kathryn hesitated, "it's rather – well, primitive?"

"Hoots!" said the driver, with rich scorn. "They hae the electric light."

"Electric light?"

"Aye. And a bathroom tu, though I'm no' sae sure of that." Again he craned over his shoulder, and his face darkened. "D'ye see the man standin' by the wee pier and lukin' at us? That'll be the Dr Colin Campbell I was tellin' ye aboot. Practices medicine in Manchester, or some sic heathen place."

The figure by the pier partly blended with the gray and brown of the landscape. It was that of a man short in stature, but very broad and burly, with a dogged, truculent lift to the shoulders. He wore an old shooting coat, with corduroy breeches and leggings, and had his hands thrust into his pockets.

It was the first time in many years that Alan had seen a doctor with a beard and mustache. These, though close-cropped, were untidy and gave an impression of shagginess together with the shaggy hair. Its color was an indeterminate brown, touched with what might have been yellow or more probably gray. Colin Campbell, the first of Angus's two younger brothers, was in his middle or late sixties, but looked younger.

He watched them critically as Alan assisted Kathryn out of the boat, and Swan scrambled after them. Though his manner was not unamiable, there was always a suggestion of a bristle about it.

"And who," he said in a heavy bass voice, "might you be?"

Alan performed introductions. Colin took his hands out of his pockets, but did not offer to shake hands.

"Well," he said, "you might as well come in. Why not? They're all here: the Fiscal, and the law-agent, and the man from the insurance company, and Uncle Tom Cobleigh and all. This is Alistair Duncan's doing, I suppose?"

"That's the solicitor?"

"Law agent," corrected Colin, with a ferocious grin which

Alan rather liked. "Law agent, when you're in Scotland. Yes. That's what I meant."

He turned to Swan, and his shaggy eyebrows drew together over a pair of leonine eyes.

"What did you say *your* name was? Swan? Swan? I don't know any Swans."

"I'm here," said Swan, as though bracing himself, "at the request of Miss Elspat Campbell."

Colin stared at him.

"Elspat sent for you?" he roared. "*Elspat?* God's wounds! I don't believe it!"

"Why not?"

"Because, barring a doctor or a minister, Aunt Elspat never sent for anything or anybody in her life. The only person or thing she ever wanted to see was my brother Angus and the London *Daily Floodlight*. God's wounds! The old girl's more cracked than ever. Reads the *Daily Floodlight* from cover to cover; knows the names of all the contributors; talks about jitterbugs and God knows what."

"The *Daily Floodlight?*" said Kathryn, with virtuous contempt. "That filthy scandal-sheet?"

"Here! Oi! Go easy!" protested Swan. "You're talking about my paper."

It was the turn of all of them to stare at him.

"You're not a reporter?" breathed Kathryn.

Swan was soothing. "Now look," he said with great earnestness. "It's all right. I'm not going to use that bit about you and Doc Campbell sleeping in the same compartment on the train: that is, unless I have to. I only –"

Colin interrupted him with a sudden and unexpected deep-throated bellow of laughter. Colin smote his knee, squared himself, and seemed to be addressing the whole universe.

"A reporter? Why not? Come in and welcome! Why not spread the story all over Manchester and London too? Do us good! And what's this about the two scholars of the family being up to hanky-panky on the train?"

"I tell you –"

"Not another word. I like you for it. God's wounds! I like to see a bit of spirit in the younger generation, the kind *we* used to have. God's wounds!"

He clapped Alan on the back, and put a heavy arm round Alan's shoulders, shaking him. His amiability was as overpowering as his truculence. Then, after roaring all this into the evening air, he lowered his voice conspiratorially.

"We can't put you in the same room here, I'm afraid. Got to keep up some of the proprieties. Let you have adjoining rooms, though. But mind you don't mention this to Aunt Elspat."

"Listen! For the love of –"

"She's a great stickler for the conventions, in spite of being Angus's mistress for forty years; and anyway, in Scotland, she's now got the status of a common-law wife. Come in! Don't stand there making funny faces! Come in! (Throw up those suitcases, Jock, and look sharp about it!)"

"Ma name's not Jock," said the oarsman, jumping up precariously in the boat.

Colin stuck out his bearded chin.

"It's Jock," he retorted, "if I say it's Jock. Just get that through your head, my lad. Do you want any money?"

"Not from you. Ma name –"

"Then that's just as well," said Colin, taking a suitcase under each arm as though they were parcels; "because damn me if I know whether I've got any to give you."

He turned to the others.

"That's the situation. If Angus was murdered, by Alec Forbes or anybody else, or if he fell out of that window by accident, then Elspat and I are rich, Elspat and a hard-working, stony broke GP are both rich. But if Angus committed suicide, I tell you straight we haven't got a penny to bless our names."

5

"But I understood –" Alan began.

"You understood the old skinflint was rich? Yes! So did everybody else. But it's the same old story." Colin's next remarks were darkly mysterious. "Ice cream!" he said. "Tractors! Drake's gold! Trust a skinflint to be a simpleton when he thinks he can get richer.

"Not that Angus was exactly a skinflint, mind. He was a swine, but a decent sort of swine, if you know what I mean. He helped me when I needed it, and he'd have helped our other brother too, if anybody'd known where to find the bounder after he got into trouble.

"Well, what are we all standing here for? Get on into the house! You – where's *your* suitcase?"

Swan, who had been vainly attempting to get in a word edgeways throughout this, gave it up for the moment as a bad job.

"I'm not staying, thanks very much," Swan replied. He turned to the driver. "You'll wait for me?"

"Aye. I'll wait."

"Then that's settled," roared Colin. "Here – you – Jock. Get round to the kitchen and tell 'em to give you a half. Angus's best whisky, mind. The rest of you, follow me."

Leaving behind them a man passionately announcing to the air that his name was not Jock, they followed Colin to the arched doorway. Swan, who appeared to have something on his mind, touched Colin's arm.

"Look," he said. "It's none of my business, but are you sure you know what you're doing?"

"Know what I'm doing? How?"

"Well," said Swan, pushing his soft gray hat to the back of his head, "I've heard the Scotch were booze-histers, of course; but this beats anything I ever expected. Is half a pint of whisky at one shot your usual tipple in these parts? He won't be able to see the road on the way back, will he?"

"A half, you ruddy Sassenach, is a small whisky. And you!" Colin now got behind Kathryn and Alan, and shooed them ahead of him. "You must have something to eat. Got to keep your strength up."

The hall into which he led them was spacious, but rather musty; and it smelt of old stone. They could make out little in the semi-gloom. Colin opened the door of a room on the left.

"Wait in there, you two," he ordered. "Swan, my lad, you come with me. I'll dig out Elspat. Elspat! *Elspat!* Where the devil are you, Elspat? Oh: and if you hear anybody arguing in the back room, that's only Duncan the law agent, and Walter Chapman from the Hercules Insurance Company."

Alone, Alan and Kathryn found themselves in a long but rather low-ceilinged room with a faintly pervading odor of damp oilcloth. A wood fire had been lit in the grate against the evening chill. By the light of the fire, and the fainter one which struggled in through the two windows facing the loch, they saw that the furniture was horsehair, the pictures large, numerous, and running to broad gilt frames, and the carpet red but faded.

On a side table lay an immense family Bible. A photograph, draped in black crepe, stood on the red tasseled cloth of the overmantel. The resemblance of the man in the photograph to

Colin, despite the fact that he was smooth-shaven and had clear white hair, left no doubt who this was.

No clock ticked. They spoke, instinctively, in whispers.

"Alan Campbell," whispered Kathryn, whose face was as pink as confectionery, "you beast!"

"Why?"

"In heaven's name, don't you realize what they're *thinking* about us? And that dreadful *Daily Floodlight* will print anything. Don't you mind at all?"

Alan considered this.

"Candidly," he startled even himself by replying, "I don't. My only regret is that it isn't true."

Kathryn fell back a little, putting her hand on the table which held the family Bible as though to support herself. He observed, however, that her color was deeper than ever.

"*Dr* Campbell! What on earth has come over you?"

"I don't know," he was honest enough to admit. "I don't know whether Scotland usually affects people like this –"

"I should hope not!"

"But I feel like taking down a claymore and stalking about with it. Also, I feel no end of an old rip and I am enjoying it. Has anyone ever told you, by the way, that you are an exceedingly attractive wench?"

"Wench? You called me a wench?"

"It is classical seventeenth-century terminology."

"But nothing like your precious Duchess of Cleveland, of course," said Kathryn.

"I acknowledge," said Alan, measuring her with an appraising eye, "a lack of proportions which would have aroused enthusiasm in Rubens. At the same time –"

"Sh-h!"

At the end of the room opposite the windows there was a partly open door. From the room beyond two voices suddenly spoke together, as though after a long silence. One voice was dry and elderly, the other voice was younger, brisker, and more suave. The voices apologized to each other. It was the younger voice which continued.

"My dear Mr Duncan," it said, "you don't seem to appreciate my position in this matter. I am merely the representative of the Hercules Insurance Company. It is my duty to investigate this claim –"

"And investigate it fairly."

"Of course. To investigate, and advise my firm whether to pay or contest the claim. There's nothing personal in it! I would do anything I could to help. I knew the late Mr Angus Campbell, and liked him."

"You knew him personally?"

"I did."

The elderly voice, which was always preceded by a strong inhalation through the nose, now spoke as with the effect of a pounce.

"Then let me put a question to you, Mr Chapman."

"Yes?"

"You would have called Mr Campbell a sane man?"

"Yes, certainly."

"A man sensible, shall we say," the voice sniffed, and became even more dry before it pounced, "to the value of money?"

"Very much so."

"Yes. Good. Very well. Now, Mr Chapman, besides his life-insurance policies with your company, my client had two policies with other companies."

"I would know nothing of that."

"But I tell you so, sir!" snapped the elderly voice, and there was a little rap as of knuckles on wood. "He held large policies with the Gibraltar Insurance Company and the Planet Insurance Company."

"Well?"

"Well! Life insurance now constitutes the whole of his assets,

Mr Chapman. The *whole* of them, sir. It was the sole one of his possessions which he was sensible enough not to throw into these mad financial ventures of his. Each one of those policies contains a suicide clause . . ."

"Naturally."

"I quite agree. Naturally! But attend to me. Three days before he died, Mr Campbell took out still another policy, with your company again, for three thousand pounds. I should – ah – imagine that the premiums, at his age, would be enormous?"

"They are naturally high. But our doctor considered Mr Campbell a first-class risk, good for fifteen years more."

"Very well. Now that," pursued Mr Alistair Duncan, law agent and Writer to the Signet, "made a grand total of some thirty-five thousand pounds in insurance."

"Indeed?"

"And each policy contained a suicide clause. Now, my good sir! My very good sir! Can you, as a man of the world, for one moment imagine that three days after he has taken out this additional policy, Angus Campbell would deliberately commit suicide and invalidate everything?"

There was a silence.

Alan and Kathryn, listening without scruple, heard someone begin slowly to walk about the floor. They could imagine the lawyer's bleak smile.

"Come, sir! Come! You are English. But I am a Scotsman, and so is the Procurator Fiscal."

"I acknowledge –"

"You *must* acknowledge it, Mr Chapman."

"But what do you suggest?"

"Murder," replied the law agent promptly. "And probably by Alec Forbes. You have heard about their quarrel. You have heard about Forbes's calling here on the night of Mr Campbell's death. You have heard about the mysterious suitcase (or dog carrier, whatever the term is), and the missing diary."

There was another silence. The slow footsteps paced up and down, carrying an atmosphere of worry. Mr Walter Chapman, of the Hercules Insurance Company, spoke in a different voice.

"But, hang it all, Mr Duncan! We just can't go on things like that!"

"No?"

"No. It's all very well to say, 'Would he have done this or that?' But, by the evidence, he *did* do it. Would you mind letting me talk for a minute?"

"Not at all."

"Right! Now, Mr Campbell usually slept in that room at the top of the tower. Correct?"

"Yes."

"On the night of his death, he was seen to retire as usual at ten o'clock, locking and bolting the door on the inside. Admitted?"

"Admitted."

"His body was found early the following morning, at the foot of the tower. He had died of a broken back and multiple injuries caused by the fall."

"Yes."

"He was not," pursued Chapman, "drugged, or overcome in any way, as the post-mortem examination showed. So an accidental fall from the window can be ruled out."

"I rule out nothing, my dear sir. But continue."

"Now as to murder. In the morning, the door was still locked and bolted on the inside. The window (you can't deny this, Mr Duncan) is absolutely inaccessible. We had a professional steeplejack over from Glasgow to look at it.

"That window is fifty-eight and a quarter feet up from the ground. There are no other windows on that side of the tower. Below is a fall of smooth stone to the pavement. Above is a conical roof of slippery slate.

"The steeplejack is willing to swear that nobody, with

46

whatever ropes or tackle, could get up to that window, or down from it again. I'll go into details, if you like –"

"That won't be necessary, my dear sir."

"But the question of somebody climbing up to that window, pushing Mr Campbell out, and climbing down again; or even hiding in the room (which nobody was) and climbing down afterwards: both these are out of the question."

He paused.

But Mr Alistair Duncan was neither impressed nor abashed.

"In that case," the law agent said, "how did that dog carrier get into the room?"

"I beg your pardon?"

The bleak voice rolled on.

"Mr Chapman, allow *me* to refresh *your* memory. At half past nine that night there had been a violent quarrel with Alec Forbes, who forced himself into the house and even into Mr Campbell's bedroom. He was – ah – ejected with difficulty."

"All right!"

"Later, both Miss Elspat Campbell and the maidservant, Kirstie MacTavish, were alarmed for fear Forbes had come back, and might have hidden himself with the intention of doing Mr Campbell some injury.

"Miss Campbell and Kirstie searched Mr Campbell's bedroom. They looked in the press, and so on. They even (as I am, ah, told is a woman's habit) looked under the bed. As you say, nobody was hiding there. But mark the fact, sir. Mark it.

"When the door of Mr Campbell's room was broken open the following morning, there was found under the bed a leather and metal object like a large suitcase, with a wire grating at one end. The sort of case which is used to contain dogs when they are taken on journeys. *Both women swear that this case was not under the bed when they looked there the night before, just before Mr Campbell locked and bolted the door on the inside.*"

The voice made an elaborate pause.

"I merely ask, Mr Chapman: how did that case get there?"

The man from the insurance company groaned.

"I repeat, sir: I merely put the question. If you will come with me, and have a word with Mr MacIntyre, the Fiscal –"

There were steps on the floor beyond. A figure came into the dim front room, ducking to avoid the rather low door-top, and touched a light-switch beside the door.

Kathryn and Alan were caught, guiltily, as the light went on. A large, brassy-stemmed chandelier, which could have contained six electric bulbs and did contain one, glowed out over their heads.

Alan's mental picture of Alistair Duncan and Walter Chapman was more or less correct except that the law agent was rather taller and leaner, and the insurance man rather shorter and broader than he had expected.

The lawyer was stoop-shouldered and somewhat nearsighted, with a large Adam's apple and grizzled hair round a pale bald spot. His collar was too large for him, but his black coat and striped trousers remained impressive.

Chapman, a fresh-faced young-looking man in a fashionably cut double-breasted suit, had a suave but very worried manner. His fair hair, smoothly brushed, shone in the light. He was the sort who, in Angus Campbell's youth, would have grown a beard at twenty-one and lived up to it ever afterwards.

"Oh, ah," said Duncan, blinking vaguely at Alan and Kathryn. "Have you – er – seen Mr MacIntyre about?"

"No, I don't think so," replied Alan, and began introductions. "Mr Duncan, we are . . ."

The law agent's eyes wandered over to another door, one facing the door to the hall.

"I should imagine, my dear sir," he continued, addressing Chapman, "that he's gone up into the tower. Will you be good enough to follow me, please?" For the last time Duncan looked back to the two newcomers. "How do you do?" he added courteously. "Good day."

And with no more words he held open the other door for Chapman to precede him. They passed through, and the door closed.

Kathryn stood staring after them.

"Well!" she began explosively. "Well!"

"Yes," admitted Alan, "he does look as though he might be a bit vague, *except* when he's talking business. But that, I submit, is the sort of lawyer you want. I'd back that gentleman any time."

"But, Dr Campbell –"

"Will you kindly stop calling me 'Dr Campbell'?"

"All right, if you insist: Alan." Kathryn's eyes were shining with a light of interest and fascination. "This situation is dreadful, and yet . . . Did you hear what they said?"

"Naturally."

"He wouldn't have committed suicide, and yet he couldn't have been murdered. It –"

She got no further, for they were interrupted by the entrance of Charles Swan from the hall. But this was a Swan with his journalistic blood up. Though usually punctilious about his manners, he had still neglected to remove his hat, which clung in some mysterious fashion to the back of his head. He walked as though on eggshells.

"Is this a story?" he demanded: a purely rhetorical question. "Is this a *story*? Holy, jumping . . . look. I didn't think there was anything in it. But my city editor – sorry; you call 'em news editors over here – thought there might be good stuff in it; and was he right?"

"Where have you been?"

"Talking to the maid. Always go for the maids first, if you can corner 'em. Now look."

Opening and shutting his hands, Swan peered round the room to make sure they were alone, and lowered his voice.

"Dr Campbell, Colin I mean, has just dug out the old lady. They're bringing her in here to put me on view."

"You haven't seen her yet?"

"No! But I've got to make a good impression if it's the last thing I ever do in my life. It ought to be a snip, because the old lady has a proper opinion of the *Daily Floodlight*, which other people" – here he looked very hard at them – "don't seem to share. But this may be good for a daily story. Cripes, the old dame might even invite me to stay at the house! What do you think?"

"I think she might. But –"

"So get set, Charley Swan, and do your stuff!" breathed Swan in the nature of a minor prayer. "We've got to keep in with her anyway, because it seems she's the autocrat of the place. So get set, you people. Dr Campbell's bringing her along here now."

6

It was unnecessary for Swan to point this out, since the voice of Aunt Elspat could already be heard outside the partly open door.

Colin Campbell spoke in a low-voiced bass rumble, of which no words were audible, evidently urging something under his breath. But Aunt Elspat, who had a particularly penetrating voice, took no trouble to lower it.

She said:

"Adjoinin' rooms! Indeed and I'll no' gie 'em adjoinin' rooms!"

The bass rumble grew more blurred, as though in protest or warning. But Aunt Elspat would have none of it.

"This is a decent, God-fearin' hoose, Colin Campbell; and a' yere sinfu' Manchester ways canna mak' it any different! Adjoinin' rooms! *Who's burnin' ma guid electric light at this time o' the day?*"

This last was delivered, in a tone of extraordinary ferocity, the moment Aunt Elspat appeared at the door.

She was a middle-sized, angular woman in a dark dress, who somehow contrived to appear larger than her actual size. Kathryn had suggested her age as "nearly ninety"; but this, Alan knew, was an error. Aunt Elspat was seventy, and a well-preserved seventy at that. She had very sharp, very restless and penetrating black eyes. She carried a copy of the *Daily Floodlight* under her arm, and her dress rustled as she walked.

Swan hastened over to extinguish the light, almost upsetting her as he did so. Aunt Elspat eyed him without favor.

"Swi' on that light again," she said curtly. "It's sae dark a body canna see. Where's Alan Campbell and Kathryn Campbell?"

Colin, now as amiable as a sportive Newfoundland, pointed them out. Aunt Elspat subjected them to a long, silent, and uncomfortable scrutiny, her eyelids hardly moving. Then she nodded.

"Aye," she said. "Ye're Campbells. *Our* Campbells." She went across to the horsehair sofa beside the table which held the family Bible, and sat down. She was wearing, evidently, boots; and not small ones.

"Him that's gone," she continued, her eyes moving to the black-draped photograph, "caud tell a Campbell, our Campbells, i' ten thousand. Aye, if he blacked his face and spoke wi' a strange tongue, Angus wad speir him."

Again she was silent for an interminable time, her eyes never leaving her visitors.

"Alan Campbell," she said abruptly, "what's yere releegion?"

"Well – Church of England, I suppose."

"Ye suppause? Dinna ye ken?"

"All right, then. It *is* Church of England."

"And that'd be your releegion tu?" Aunt Elspat demanded of Kathryn.

"Yes, it is!"

Aunt Elspat nodded as though her darkest suspicions were confirmed.

"Ye dinna gang tae the kirk. I kenned it." She said this in a shivering kind of voice, and suddenly got steam up. "Rags o' Popery!" she said. "Think shame tae yereself, Alan Campbell, think shame and sorrow tae yere ain kith and kin, that wad dally wi' sin and lechery i' the hoose of the Scairlet Woman!"

Swan was shocked at such language.

"Now, ma'am, I'm sure he never goes to places like that," Swan protested, defending Alan. "And, besides, you could hardly call this young lady a –"

Aunt Elspat turned round.

"Who's yon," she asked, pointing her finger at Swan, "wha' burns ma guid electric light at this time o' the day?"

"Ma'am, I didn't –"

"Who's yon?"

Taking a deep breath, Swan assumed his most winning smile and stepped in front of her.

"Miss Campbell, I represent the *Daily Floodlight*, that paper you've got there. My editor was very pleased to get your letter; pleased that we've got appreciative readers all over this broad country. Now, Miss Campbell, you said in your letter that you had some sensational disclosures to make about a crime that was committed here –"

"Eh?" roared Colin Campbell, turning to stare at her.

"And my editor sent me all the way from London to interview you. I'd be very pleased to hear anything you'd like to tell me, either on or off the record."

Cupping one hand behind her ear, Aunt Elspat listened with the same unwinking, beady stare. At length she spoke.

"So ye're an American, eh?" she said, and her eye began to gleam. "Hae ye heard –"

This was much to bear, but Swan braced himself and smiled.

"Yes, Miss Campbell," he said patiently. "You don't need to tell me. I know. I've heard all about your brother Angus, who wouldn't even give the bloodhounds a penny."

Swan stopped abruptly.

He seemed to realize, in a vague kind of way, that he had made a slip somewhere, and that his version of the anecdote was not quite correct.

"I mean –" he began.

Both Alan and Kathryn were looking at him not without interested curiosity. But the most pronounced effect was on Aunt Elspat. She merely sat and stared at Swan. He must have realized that she was staring fixedly at the hat still on his head, for he snatched it off.

Presently Elspat spoke. Her words, slow and weighty as a judge's summing-up, fell with measured consideration.

"Any why should Angus Campbell gie the bluidhoonds a penny?"

"I mean –"

"It wadna be muckle use tae them, wad it?"

"I mean, *cent!*"

"Sent wha'?"

"C-e-n-t, cent."

"In ma opeenion, young man," said Aunt Elspat, after a long pause, "ye're a bug-hoose. Gie'in' siller tae bluidhoonds!"

"I'm sorry, Miss Campbell! Skip it! It was a joke."

Of all the unfortunate words he could have used in front of Aunt Elspat, this was the worst. Even Colin was now glaring at him.

"Joke, is it?" said Elspat, gradually getting steam up again. "Angus Campbell scarce cauld in his coffin, and ye'd come insultin' a hoose o' mournin' wi' yere godless *jokes?* I'll no' stand it! In ma opeenion, ye skellum, ye didna come fra the *Daily Floodlight* at all. Who's Pip Emma?" she flung at him.

"Pardon?"

"Who's Pip Emma? Ah! Ye dinna ken that either, du ye?" cried Aunt Elspat, flourishing the paper. "Ye dinna ken the lass wha' writes the column i' ye're ain paper! Dinna fash yeresel' tae mak' excuses! – What's yere name?"

"MacHolster."

"Wha'?"

"MacHolster," said the scion of that improbable clan, now so rattled by Aunt Elspat that his usually nimble wits had deserted him. "I mean, MacQueen. What I mean is: it's really Swan, Charles Evans Swan, but I'm descended from the MacHolsters or the MacQueens – and –"

Aunt Elspat did not even comment on this. She merely pointed to the door.

"But I tell you, Miss Campbell –"

"Gang your ways," said Aunt Elspat. "I'll no' tell ye twice."

"You heard what she said, young fellow," interposed Colin, putting his thumbs in the armholes of his waistcoat and turning a fierce gaze on the visitor. "God's wounds! I wanted to be hospitable, but there are some things we don't joke about in this house."

"But I swear to you –"

"Now will you go by the door," inquired Colin, lowering his hands, "or will you go by the window?"

For a second Alan thought Colin was really going to take the visitor by the collar and the slack of the trousers, and run him through the house like a chucker-out at a pub.

Swan, breathing maledictions, reached the door two seconds before Colin. They heard him make a speedy exit. The whole thing was over so quickly that Alan could hardly realize what had happened. But the effect on Kathryn was to reduce her almost to the verge of tears.

"What a family!" she cried, clenching her fists and stamping her foot on the floor. "Oh, good heavens, what a family!"

"And wha' ails *you*, Kathryn Campbell?"

Kathryn was a fighter.

"Do you want to know what I really think, Aunt Elspat?"

"Weel?"

"I think you're a very silly old woman, that's what I think. Now throw me out too."

To Alan's surprise, Aunt Elspat smiled.

"Maybe no' sae daft, ma dear," she said complacently, and smoothed her skirt. "Maybe no' sae daft!"

"What do you think, Alan?"

"I certainly don't think you should have chucked him out like that. At least, not without asking to see his press card. The fellow's perfectly genuine. But he's like the man in Shaw's *The Doctor's Dilemma:* congenitally incapable of reporting accurately anything he sees or hears. He may be able to make a lot of trouble."

"Trouble?" demanded Colin. "How?"

"I don't know, but I have my suspicions."

Colin's bark was, obviously, very much worse than his bite. He ran a hand through his shaggy mane of hair, glared, and ended by scratching his nose.

"Look here," he growled. "Do you think I ought to go out and fetch the fellow back? Got some eighty-year-old whisky here, that'd make a donkey sing. We'll tap it tonight, Alan, my lad. If we fed him that –"

Aunt Elspat put her foot down with a calm, implacable arrogance that was like granite.

"I'll no' hae the skellum in ma hoose."

"I know, old girl; but –"

"I'm tellin' ye: I'll no' hae the skellum in ma hoose. That's all. I'll write tae the editor again –"

Colin glared at her. "Yes, but that's what I wanted to ask you. What's all this tommy-rot about mysterious secrets you will tell the newspapers but won't tell us?"

Elspat shut her lips mulishly.

"Come on!" said Colin. "Come clean!"

"Colin Campbell," said Elspat, with slow and measured vindictiveness, "du as I tell ye. Tak' Alan Campbell up tae the tower, and let him see how Angus Campbell met a bad end. Let him think o' Holy Writ. You, Kathryn Campbell, sit by me." She patted the sofa. "Du ye gang tae the godless dance halls o' London, noo?"

"Certainly not!" said Kathryn.

"Then ye hae never seen a jitterbug?"

What might have come of this improving conversation Alan never learned. Colin impelled him toward the door across the room, where Duncan and Chapman had disappeared a while ago.

It opened, Alan saw, directly into the ground floor of the tower. It was a big, round, gloomy room, with stone walls whitewashed on the inside, and an earth floor. You might have suspected that at one time it had been used for stabling. Wooden double doors, with a chain and padlock, opened out into the court on the south side.

These now stood open, letting in what light there was. In the wall was a low-arched door, giving on a spiral stone stair which climbed up inside the tower.

"Somebody's always leaving these doors open," growled Colin. "Padlock on the outside, too, if you can believe that! Anybody who got a duplicate key could . . .

"Look here, my lad. The old girl knows something. God's wounds! She's not daft; you saw that. But she knows something. And yet she keeps her lip buttoned, in spite of the fact that thirty-five thousand pounds in insurance may hang on it."

"Can't she even tell the police?"

Colin snorted.

"Police? Man, she can't even be civil to the Procurator Fiscal, let alone the regular police! She had some row with 'em a long time ago – about a cow, or I don't know what – and she's convinced they're all thieves and villains. That's the reason for this newspaper business, I imagine."

From his pocket Colin fished out a briar pipe and an oilskin pouch. He filled the pipe and lit it. The glow of the match illumined his shaggy beard and mustache, and the fierce eyes which acquired a cross-eyed expression as he stared at the burning tobacco.

"As for me . . . well, that doesn't matter so much. I'm an old war-horse. I've got my debts; and Angus knew it; but I can pull through somehow. Or at least I hope I can. But Elspat! Not a farthing! God's wounds!"

"How is the money divided?"

"Provided we get it, you mean?"

"Yes."

"That's simple. Half to me, and half to Elspat."

"Under her status as his common-law wife?"

"Sh-h!" thundered the quiet Colin, and looked round quickly, and waved the shriveled match-end at his companion. "Slip of the tongue. She'll never put in a claim to be his common-law wife: you can bet your boots on that. The old girl's passion for respectability verges on the morbid. I told you that."

"I should have gathered it, somehow."

"She'll never admit she was more than his 'relative,' not in thirty years. Even Angus, who was a free-spoken devil, never alluded to it in public. No, no, no. The money is a straight bequest. Which we're never likely to get."

He flung away the spent match. He squared his shoulders, and nodded toward the staircase.

"Well! Come on. That is, if you feel up to it. There's five floors above this, and a hundred and four steps to the top. But come on. Mind your head."

Alan was too fascinated to bother about the number of steps.

But they seemed interminable, as a winding stair always does. The staircase was lighted at intervals along the west side – that is, the side away from the loch – by windows which had been hacked out to larger size. It had a musty, stably smell, not improved by the savor of Colin's pipe tobacco.

In daylight that was almost gone, making walking difficult on the uneven stone humps, they groped up along the outer face of the wall.

"But your brother didn't always sleep clear up at the top, did he?" Alan inquired.

"Yes, indeed. Every night for years. Liked the view out over the loch. Said the air was purer too, though that's all my eye. God's wounds! I'm out of condition!"

"Does anybody occupy any of these other rooms?"

"No. Just full of junk. Relics of Angus's get-rich-quick-and-be-happy schemes."

Colin paused, puffing, at a window on the last landing but one.

And Alan looked out. Remnants of red sunset lay still ghostly among the trees. Though they could not have been so very high up, yet the height seemed immense.

Below them, westwards, lay the main road to Inveraray. Up the Glen of Shira, and, farther on, the fork where Glen Aray ascended in deep hills toward Dalmally, were tangled stretches where the fallen timber now rotted and turned gray. It marked the track, Colin said, of the great storm which had swept Argyllshire a few years back. It was a wood of the dead, even of dead trees.

Southwards, above the spiky pines, you could see far away the great castle of Argyll, with the four great towers whose roofs change color when it rains. Beyond would be the estate office, once the courthouse, where James Stewart, guardian of Alan Breck Stewart, had been tried and condemned for the Appin murder. All the earth was rich and breathing with names, with songs, with tradition, with superstitions –

"Dr Campbell," said Alan, very quietly, "how did the old man die?"

Sparks flew from Colin's pipe.

"You ask me? *I* don't know. Except that he never committed suicide. Angus kill himself? Hoots!"

More sparks flew from the pipe.

"I don't want to see Alec Forbes hang," he added querulously; "but he's ruddy well got to hang. Alec 'ud have cut Angus's heart out and never thought twice about it."

"Who is this Alec Forbes?"

"Oh, some bloke who came and settled here, and drinks too much, and thinks he's an inventor too, in a small way. He and Angus collaborated on one idea. With the result usual to collaboration: bust-up. He said Angus cheated him. Probably Angus did."

"So Forbes came in here and cut up a row on the night of the – murder?"

"Yes. Came clear up to Angus's bedroom here, and wanted to have it out. Drunk, as like as not."

"But they cleared him out, didn't they?"

"They did. Or rather Angus did. Angus was no soft 'un, for all his years and weight. Then the womenfolk joined in, and *they* had to search the bedroom and even the other rooms to make sure Alec hadn't sneaked back."

"Which, evidently, he hadn't."

"Right. Then Angus locks his door – *and* bolts it. In the night, something happens."

If his fingernails had been longer, Colin would have gnawed at them.

"The police surgeon put the time of death as not earlier than ten o'clock and not later than one. What the hell good is that? Eh? We know he didn't die before ten o'clock anyway, because that's the last time he was seen alive. But the police surgeon wouldn't be more definite. He said Angus's injuries wouldn't have killed him instantly, so he might have been unconscious but alive for some time before death.

"Anyway, we do know that Angus had gone to bed when all this happened."

"How do we know that?"

Colin made a gesture of exasperation.

"Because he was in his nightshirt when they found him. And the bed was rumpled. And he'd put out the light and taken down the blackout from the window."

Alan was brought up with something of a start.

"Do you know," Alan muttered, "I'd almost forgotten there was a war going on, and even the question of the blackout? But look here!" He swept his hand toward the window. "*These* windows aren't blacked out?"

"No. Angus could go up and down here in the dark. He said blackouts for 'em were a waste of money. But a light showing up in that room could have been seen for miles, as even Angus had to admit. God's wounds, don't ask me so many questions! Come and see the room for yourself."

He knocked out his pipe and ran like an ungainly baboon up the remaining stairs.

7

Alistair Duncan and Walter Chapman were still arguing.

"My dear sir," said the tall, stoop-shouldered lawyer, waving a pince-nez in the air as though he were conducting an orchestra, "surely it is now obvious that this is a case of murder?"

"No."

"But the suitcase, sir! The suitcase, or dog carrier, which was found under the bed after the murder?"

"After the death."

"For the sake of clearness, shall we say murder?"

"All right: without prejudice. By what I want to know, Mr Duncan, is: what *about* that dog carrier? It was empty. It didn't contain a dog. Microscopic examination by the police showed that it hadn't contained *anything*. What is it supposed to prove anyway?"

Both of them broke off at the entrance of Alan and Colin.

The room at the top of the tower was round and spacious, though somewhat low of ceiling in comparison to its diameter. Its one door, which opened in from a little landing, had its lock torn out from the frame; and the staple of the bolt, still rustily embedded round the bolt, was also wrenched loose.

The one window, opposite the door, exerted over Alan an ugly fascination.

It was larger than it had seemed from the ground. It consisted of two leaves, opening out like little doors after the fashion of windows in France, and of leaded-glass panes in diamond shapes. It was clearly a modern addition, the original window having been enlarged; and was, Alan thought, dangerously low.

Seen thus in the gloaming, a luminous shape in a cluttered room, it took the eye with a kind of hypnosis. But it was the only modern thing here, except for the electric bulb over the desk and the electric heater beside the desk.

A huge uncompromising oak bedstead, with a double feather bed and a crazy-quilt cover, stood against one rounded wall. There was an oak press nearly as high as the room. Some effort had been made toward cheerfulness by plastering the walls and papering them with blue cabbages in yellow joinings.

There were pictures, mainly family photographs going back as far as the fifties or sixties. The stone floor was covered with straw matting. A marble-topped dressing-table, with a gaunt mirror, had been crowded in beside a big rolltop desk bristling with papers. More correspondence, bales of it, lined the walls and set the rocking chairs at odd angles. Though there were many trade magazines, you saw no books except a Bible and a postcard album.

It was an old man's room. A pair of Angus's button boots, out of shape from bunions, still stood under the bed.

And Colin seemed to feel the reminder.

"Evening," he said, half bristling again. "This is Alan Campbell, from London. Where's the Fiscal?"

Alistair Duncan put on his pince-nez.

"Gone, I fear, home," he replied. "I suspect him of avoiding Aunt Elspat. Our young friend here" – smiling bleakly, he reached out and tapped Chapman on the shoulder – "avoids her like the plague and won't go near her."

"Well, you never know where you are with her. I deeply sympathize with her, and all that; but hang it all!"

The law agent drew together his stooped shoulders, and gloomed down on Alan.

"Haven't we met before, sir?"

"Yes. A little while ago."

"Ah! Yes. Did we – exchange words?"

"Yes. You said, 'How do you do?' and, 'Good-bye.'"

"Would," said the law agent, shaking his head, "would that all our social relations were so uncomplicated! How do you do?" He shook hands, with a bony palm and a limp grasp.

"Of course," he went on. "I remember now. I wrote to you. It was very good of you to come."

"May I ask, Mr Duncan, why you wrote to me?"

"Pardon?"

"I'm very glad to be here. I know I should have made my acquaintance with our branch of the family long before this. But neither Kathryn Campbell nor I seem to serve any very useful purpose. What did you mean, precisely, by a 'family conference'?"

"I will tell you," Duncan spoke promptly, and (for him) almost cheerfully. "Let me first present Mr Chapman, of the Hercules Life Insurance Company. A stubborn fellow."

"Mr Duncan's a bit stubborn himself," smiled Chapman.

"We have here a clear case of accident or murder," pursued the lawyer. "Have you heard the details of your unfortunate relative's death?"

"Some of them," Alan answered. "But –"

He walked forward to the window.

The two leaves were partly open. There was no upright bar or support between them: making, when the leaves were pushed open, an open space some three feet wide by four feet high. A magnificent view stretched out over the darkling water and the purple-brown hills, but Alan did not look at it.

"May I ask a question?" he said.

Colin cast up his eyes with the expression of one who says, "Another one!" But Chapman made a courteous gesture.

"By all means."

Beside the window on the floor stood its blackout: a sheet of oilcloth nailed to a light wooden frame, which fitted flat against the window.

"Well," continued Alan, indicating this, "could he have fallen out accidentally while he was taking down the blackout?"

"You know what we all do. Before climbing into bed, we turn out the light, and then grope across to take down the blackout and open the window.

"If you accidentally leaned too hard on this window while you were opening the catch, you might pitch straight forward out of it. There's no bar between."

To his surprise Duncan looked annoyed and Chapman smiled.

"Look at the thickness of the wall," suggested the man from the insurance company. "It's three feet thick: good old feudal wall. No. He couldn't possibly have done that unless he were staggering drunk or drugged or overcome in some way; and the post-mortem examination proved, as even Mr Duncan will admit –"

He glanced inquiringly at the lawyer, who grunted.

"– proved that he was none of these things. He was a sharp-eyed, surefooted old man in full possession of his senses."

Chapman paused.

"Now, gentlemen, while we're all here, I may as well make clear to all of you why I don't see how this can be anything but suicide. I should like to ask Mr Campbell's brother a question."

"Well?" said Colin sharply.

"It's true, isn't it, that Mr Angus Campbell was what we'll call a gentleman of the old school? That is, he always slept with the windows closed?"

"Yes, that's true," admitted Colin, and shoved his hands into the pockets of his shooting coat.

"I can't understand it myself," said the man from the insurance company, puffing out his lips. "I should have a head like a balloon if I ever did that. But my grandfather always did; wouldn't let in a breath of night air.

"And Mr Campbell did too. The only reason he ever took the blackout down at night was so that he should know when it was morning.

"Gentlemen, I ask you now! When Mr Campbell went to bed that night, this window was closed and its catch locked as usual. Miss Campbell and Kirstie MacTavish admit that. Later the police found Mr Campbell's fingerprints, *and only Mr Campbell's fingerprints, on the catch of that window.*

"What he did is pretty clear. At some time after ten he undressed, put on his nightshirt, took down the blackout, and went to bed as usual." Chapman pointed to the bed. "The bed is made now, but it was rumpled then."

Alistair Duncan sniffed.

"That," he said, "is Aunt Elspat's doing. She said she thought it was only decent to redd up the room."

Chapman's gesture called for silence.

"At some time between then and one o'clock in the morning he got up, walked to the window, opened it, and deliberately threw himself out.

"Hang it all, I appeal to Mr Campbell's brother! My firm wants to do the right thing. *I* want to do the right thing. As I was telling Mr Duncan, I knew the late Mr Campbell personally. He came in to see me at our Glasgow office, and took out his last policy. After all, you know, it's not *my* money. I'm not paying it out. If I could see my way clear to advise my firm to honor this claim, I'd do it like a shot. But can you honestly say the evidence warrants that?"

There was silence.

Chapman finished almost on a note of eloquence. Then he picked up his briefcase and bowler hat from the desk.

"The dog carrier –" began Duncan.

Chapman's color went up.

"Oh, damn the dog carrier!" he said, with unprofessional impatience. "Can you, sir – can any of you – suggest any reason for the dog carrier to figure in this business at all?"

Colin Campbell, bristling, went across to the bed. He reached underneath and fished out the object in question, which he regarded as though he were about to give it a swift kick.

It was about the size of a large suitcase, though somewhat wider, in box-shape. Made of dark-brown leather, it had a handle like a suitcase, but two metal clasps on the upper side. An oblong grating of wire at one end had been inset for the purpose of giving air to whatever pet might be carried.

To whatever pet might be carried . . .

In the mind of Alan Campbell there stirred a fancy so grotesque and ugly, even if unformed, as to come with a flavor of definite evil in the old tower room.

"You don't suppose," Alan heard himself saying, "he might have been frightened into doing what he did?"

His three companions whirled round.

"Frightened?" repeated the lawyer.

Alan stared at the leather box.

"I don't know anything about this man Alec Forbes," he went on, "but he seems to be a pretty ugly customer."

"Well, my dear sir?"

"Suppose Alec Forbes brought that box along with him when he came here. It'd look like an ordinary suitcase. Suppose he came here deliberately, pretending to want to 'have it out' with Angus, but really to leave the box behind. He distracts Angus's attention, and shoves the box under the bed. In the row Angus doesn't remember the suitcase afterwards. But in the middle of the night something gets out of the box . . ."

Even Alistair Duncan had begun to look a trifle uncomfortable.

And Chapman was eyeing Alan with an interest which all his skeptical and smiling incredulity could not conceal.

"Oh, see here!" he protested. "What are you suggesting, exactly?"

Alan stuck it out.

"I don't want you to laugh. But what I was actually thinking about was – well, a big spider or a poisonous snake of some kind. It would have been bright moonlight that night, remember."

Again the silence stretched out interminably. It was now so dark that they could barely see.

"It is an extraordinary thing," murmured the lawyer in his thin, dry voice. "Just one moment."

He felt in the inside pocket of his coat. From this he took a worn leather notebook. Carrying it to the window, and adjusting his pince-nez, he cocked his head at an angle to examine one page of the notebook.

"'Extracts from the statement of Kirstie MacTavish, maid-servant,'" he read, and cleared his throat. "Translated from the Doric and rendered into English, listen to this:

"Mr Campbell said to me and Miss Campbell, "Go to bed and let's have no more nonsense. I have got rid of the blellum. Did you see that suitcase he had with him, though?" We said we had not, as we did not arrive until Mr Campbell had put Mr Forbes out of the house. Mr Campbell said: "I will bet you he is leaving the country to get away from his creditors. But I wonder what he did with the suitcase? He was using two hands to try to hit me when he left.""'

Duncan peered over his pince-nez.

"Any comments on that, my dear sir?" he inquired.

The insurance agent was not amused.

"Aren't you forgetting what you pointed out to me yourself? When Miss Campbell and the maid searched this room just before Mr Campbell retired, they saw no suitcase under the bed."

Duncan rubbed his jaw. In that light he had a corpse-like, cadaverous pallor, and his grizzled hair looked like wire.

"True," he admitted. "True. At the same time –"

He shook his head.

"Snakes!" snorted the insurance agent. "Spiders! Dr Fu Manchu! Look here! Do you know of any snake or spider that could climb out of its box, and then carefully close the clasps of the box afterwards? Both clasps on that thing were found fastened on the following morning."

"That would certainly appear to be a stumbling block," conceded Duncan. "At the same time –"

"And what happened to the thing afterwards?"

"It wouldn't be very pleasant," grinned Colin Campbell, "if the thing were still here in the room somewhere."

Mr Walter Chapman hurriedly put on his bowler hat.

"I must go," he said. "Sorry, gentlemen, but I'm very late as it is and I've got to get back to Dunoon. Can I give you a lift, Mr Duncan?"

"Nonsense," roared Colin. "You're staying to tea. Both of you."

Chapman blinked at him.

"Tea? Great Scott, what time do you have your dinner?"

"You'll get no dinner, my lad. But the tea will be bigger than most dinners you ever ate. And I've got some very potent whisky I've been aching to try out on somebody, beginning with a ruddy Englishman. What do you say?"

"Sorry. Decent of you, but I must go." Chapman slapped at the sleeves of his coat. Exasperation radiated from him. "What with snakes and spiders – *and* the supernatural on top of it –"

If the scion of the MacHolsters could have chosen no more unfortunate word than "joke" in addressing Elspat Campbell, Chapman himself in addressing Colin could have chosen no more unfortunate word than "supernatural."

Colin's big head hunched down into his big shoulders.

"And who says this was supernatural?" he inquired in a soft voice.

Chapman laughed.

"*I* don't, naturally. That's a bit outside my firm's line. But the people hereabouts seem to have an idea that this place is haunted; or at least that there's something not quite right about it."

"Oh?"

"And, if I may say so without offense" – the insurance agent's eye twinkled – "they seem not to have a very high opinion of you people here. They mutter, 'a bad lot,' or something of the sort."

"We are a bad lot. God's wounds!" cried the atheistical doctor, not without pride. "Who's ever denied it? Not me. But haunted! Of all the . . . look here. You don't think Alec Forbes went about carrying a bogle in a dog box?"

"I don't think, frankly," retorted Chapman, "that anybody carried anything in any box." His worried look returned. "All the same, I should feel better if we could have a word with this Mr Forbes."

"Where is he, by the way?" asked Alan.

The law agent, who had shut up his notebook and was listening with a dry, quiet smile, struck in again.

"That, too, is an extraordinary thing. Even Mr Chapman would admit something suspicious – something just a trifle suspicious – about Alec Forbes's conduct. For, you see, Alec Forbes can't be found."

8

"You mean," asked Alan, "he did go away to escape his creditors?"

Duncan waved the pince-nez.

"Slander. No: I merely state the fact. Or he may be on a spree, which is possible. All the same, it is curious. Eh, my dear Chapman? It is *curious.*"

The insurance agent drew a deep breath.

"Gentlemen," he said, "I'm afraid I can't argue the matter any further now. I'm going to get out of here before I break my neck on those stairs in the dark.

"Here is all I am able to tell you now. I'll have a word with the Fiscal tomorrow. He must have decided by now whether he thinks this is suicide, accident, or murder. On what he does must necessarily depend what *we* do. Can I say any fairer than that?"

"Thank you. No, that will suit us. All we ask is a little time."

"But if you're sure this is murder," interposed Alan, "why doesn't your Fiscal take some real steps about it? For instance, why doesn't he call in Scotland Yard?"

Duncan regarded him with real horror.

"Summon Scotland Yard to Scotland?" he expostulated. "My dear sir!"

"I should have thought this would have been the very place for 'em," said Alan. "Why not?"

"My dear sir, it is never done! Scots law has a procedure all its own."

"By George, it has!" declared Chapman, slapping his brief case against his leg. "I've only been up here a couple of months, but I've found that out already."

"Then what are you going to do?"

"While all the rest of you," observed Colin, throwing out his barrel chest, "have been doing nothing but fiddle-faddling about and talking, other people haven't been idle. I won't tell you what I'm going to do. I'll tell you what I *have* done." His eye dared them to say it wasn't a good idea. "I've sent for Gideon Fell."

Duncan clucked his tongue thoughtfully.

"That's the man who –?"

"It is. And a good friend of mine."

"Have you thought of the – ah – expense?"

"God's wounds, can't you stop thinking about money for five seconds? Just five seconds? Anyway, it won't cost you a penny. He's coming up here as my guest, that's all. You offer him money and there'll be trouble."

The lawyer spoke stiffly.

"We all know, my dear Colin, that your own contempt for the monetary side has not failed to prove embarrassing to you at times." His glance was charged with meaning. "You must allow *me*, however, to think of the pounds, shilling, and pence. Awhile ago this gentleman" – he nodded toward Alan – "asked why this 'family conference' had been summoned. I'll tell you. If the insurance companies refuse to pay up, proceedings must be instituted. Those proceedings may be expensive."

"Do you mean to say," said Colin, his eyes starting out of their sockets, "that you brought those two kids clear up from London just in the hope they'd contribute to the basket? God's wounds, do you want your ruddy neck wrung?"

Duncan was very white.

"I am not in the habit of being talked to like that, Colin Campbell."

"Well, you're *being* talked to like that, Alistair Duncan. What do you think of it?"

For the first time a personal note crept into the law-agent's voice.

"Colin Campbell, for forty-two years I've been at the beck and call of your family –"

"Ha ha ha!"

"Colin Campbell –"

"Here! I say!" protested Chapman, so uncomfortable that he shifted from one foot to the other.

Alan also intervened by putting his hand on Colin's shivering shoulder. In another moment, he was afraid, Colin might be running a second person out of the house by the collar and the slack of the trousers.

"Excuse me," Alan said, "but my father left me pretty well off, and if there *is* anything I can do . . ."

"So? Your father left you pretty well off?" said Colin. "And well you knew it, didn't you, Alistair Duncan?"

The lawyer sputtered. What he attempted to say, so far as Alan could gather, was "Do you wish me to wash my hands of this matter?" What he actually said was something like, "Do you wash me to wish my hands of this matter?" But both he and Colin were so angry that neither noticed it.

"Yes, I do," said Colin. "That's just what I smacking well do. Now shall we go downstairs?"

In silence, with aching dignity, the quartet stumbled and blundered and groped down some very treacherous stairs. Chapman attempted to lighten matters by asking Duncan if he would care for a lift in the former's car, an offer which was accepted, and a few observations about the weather.

These fell flat.

Still in silence, they went through into the sitting-room on the ground floor, now deserted, and to the front door. As Colin and the law agent said good night, they could not have been more on their dignity had they been going to fight a duel in the morning. The door closed.

"Elspat and little Kate," said Colin, moodily smoldering, "will be having their tea. Come on."

Alan liked the dining-room, and would have liked it still more if he had not felt so ruffled.

Under a low-hanging lamp which threw bright light on the white tablecloth, with a roaring fire in the chimney, Aunt Elspat and Kathryn sat at a meal composed of sausages, Ulster fry, eggs, potatoes, tea, and enormous quantities of buttered toast.

"Elspat," said Colin, moodily drawing out a chair, "Alistair Duncan's given notice again."

Aunt Elspat helped herself to butter.

"A'weel," she said philosophically, "it's no' the fairst time, and it'll no' be the last. He gie'd me notice tu, a week syne."

Alan's intense discomfort began to lighten.

"Do you mean to say," Alan demanded, "that the business wasn't – wasn't serious?"

"Oh, no. He'll be all right in the morning," said Colin. Stirring uncomfortably, he glowered at the well-filled table. "You know, Elspat, I've got a bloody temper. I wish I could control it."

Aunt Elspat then flew out at him.

She said she would not have such profane language used in her house, and especially in front of the child: by which she presumably meant Kathryn. She further rated them for being late for tea, in terms which would have been violent had they missed two meals in a row and emptied the soup over her at the third.

Alan only half listened. He was beginning to understand Aunt Elspat a little better now, and to realize that her outbursts were almost perfunctory. Long ago Aunt Elspat had been compelled to fight and fight to get her own way in all things; and continued it, as a matter of habit, long after it had ceased to be necessary. It was not even bad temper: it was automatic.

The walls of the dining-room were ornamented with withered stags' heads, and there were two crossed claymores over the chimneypiece. They attracted Alan. A sense of well-being stole into him as he devoured his food, washing it down with strong black tea.

"Ah!" said Colin, with an expiring sigh. He pushed back his chair, stretched, and patted his stomach. His face glowed out of the beard and shaggy hair. "Now that's better. That's very much better. Rot me if I don't feel like ringing up the old weasel and apologizing to him!"

"Did you," said Kathryn hesitantly, "did you find out anything? Up there in the tower? Or decide on anything?"

Colin inserted a toothpick into his beard.

"No, Kitty-kat, we didn't."

"And please don't call me Kitty-kat! You all treat me as though I weren't grown-up!"

"Hoots!" said Aunt Elspat, giving her a withering look. "Ye're *not* grown-up."

"We didn't decide on anything," pursued Colin, continuing to pat his stomach. "But then we didn't need to. Gideon Fell'll be here tomorrow. In fact, I thought it was Fell coming when I saw your boat tonight. And when *he* gets here –"

"Did you say Fell?" cried Kathryn. "Not Dr Fell?"

"That's the chap."

"Not that horrible man who writes letters to the newspapers? *You* know, Alan!"

"He's a very distinguished scholar, Kitty-kat," said Colin, "and as such you ought to take off your wee bonnet to him. But his main claims to notoriety lie along the line of detecting crime."

Aunt Elspat wanted to know what his religion was.

Colin said he didn't know, but that it didn't matter a damn *what* his religion was.

Aunt Elspat intimated, on the contrary, that it mattered very much indeed, adding remarks which left her listeners in no doubt about her views touching Colin's destination in the after-life. This, to Alan, was the hardest part of Elspat's discourse to put up with. Her notions of theology were childish. Her knowledge of Church history would have been considered inaccurate even by the late Bishop Burnet. But good manners kept him silent, until he could get in a relevant question.

"The only part I haven't got quite clear," he said, "is about the diary."

Aunt Elspat stopped hurling damnation right and left, and applied herself to her tea.

"Diary?" repeated Colin.

"Yes. I'm not even sure if I heard properly; it might refer to something else. But, when Mr Duncan and the insurance fellow were talking in the next room, we heard Mr Duncan say something about a 'missing diary.' At least, that's how I understood it."

"And so did I," agreed Kathryn.

Colin scowled.

"As far as I can gather" – he put a finger on his napkin ring, sending it spinning out on the table to roll back to him – "somebody pinched it, that's all."

"What diary?"

"*Angus's* diary, dammit! He carefully kept one every year, and at the end of the year burned it so that nobody should ever find it and know what he was really thinking."

"Prudent habit."

"Yes. Well, he wrote it up every night just before he went to bed. Never knew him to miss. It should have been on the desk next morning. But – at least, so they tell me – it wasn't. Eh, Elspat?"

"Drink your tea and dinna be sae daft."

Colin sat up.

"What the devil's daft about that? The diary wasn't there, was it?"

Carefully, with ladylike daintiness which showed she knew her manners, Elspat poured tea into the saucer, blew on it, and drank.

"The trouble is," Colin continued, "that nobody even noticed the absence of the diary until a good many hours afterwards. So anybody who saw it lying there could have pinched it in the meantime. I mean, there's no proof that the phantom murderer got it. It might have been anybody. Eh, Elspat?"

Aunt Elspat regarded the empty saucer for a moment, and then sighed.

"I suppause," she said resignedly, "you'll be wantin' the whisky, noo?"

Colin's face lit up.

"Now there," he boomed with fervency, "there, in the midst of this mess, is the idea that the world's been waiting for!" He turned to Alan. "Lad, would you like to taste some mountain dew that'll take the top of your head off? Would you?"

The dining-room was snug and warm, though the wind rose outside. As always in the presence of Kathryn, Alan felt expansive and on his mettle.

"It would be very interesting," he replied, settling back, "to find any whisky that could take the top of my head off."

"Oho? You think so, do you?"

"You must remember," said Alan, not without reason on his side, "that I spent three years in the United States during prohibition days. Anybody who can survive *that* experience has nothing to fear from any liquor that ever came out of a still – or didn't."

"You think so, eh?" mused Colin. "Do you now? Well, well, well! Elspat, this calls for heroic measures. Bring out the Doom of the Campbells."

Elspat rose without protest.

"A'weel," she said, "I've seen it happen befair. It'll happen again when I'm gone. I caud du wi' a wee nip masel', the nicht bein' cauld."

She creaked out of the room, and returned bearing a decanter nearly full of a darkish brown liquid filled with gold where the light struck it. Colin placed it tenderly on the table. For Elspat and Kathryn he poured out an infinitesimal amount. For himself and Alan he poured out about a quarter of a tumblerful.

"How will you have it, lad?"

"American style. Neat, with water on the side."

"Good! Damn good!" roared Colin. "You don't want to spoil it. Now drink up. Go on. Drink it."

They – or at least Colin and Elspat – were regarding him with intense interest. Kathryn sniffed suspiciously at the liquid in her glass, but evidently decided that she liked it. Colin's face was red and of a violent eagerness, his eyes wide open and mirth lurking in his soul.

"To happier days," said Alan.

He lifted the glass, drained it, and almost literally reeled.

It did not take the top of his head off; but for a second he thought it was going to. The stuff was strong enough to make a battleship alter its course. The veins of his temples felt bursting; his eyesight dimmed; and he decided that he must be strangling to death. Then, after innumerable seconds, he opened swimming eyes to find Colin regarding him with proud glee.

Next, something else happened.

Once that spiritous bomb had exploded, and he could recover breath and eyesight, a fey sense of exhilaration and well-being crawled along his veins. The original buzzing in the head was succeeded by a sense of crystal clearness, the feeling which Newton or Einstein must have felt at the approaching solution of a complex mathematical problem.

He had kept himself from coughing, and the moment passed.

"Well?" demanded Colin.

"Aaah!" said his guest.

"Here's to happier days too!" thundered Colin, and drained his own glass. The effects here were marked as well, though Colin recovered himself a shade more quickly.

Then Colin beamed on him. "Like it?"

"I do!"

"Not too strong for you?"

"No."

"Care for another?"

"Thanks. I don't mind if I do."

"A'weel!" said Elspat resignedly. "A'weel!"

Alan Campbell opened one eye.

From somewhere in remote distances, muffled beyond sight or sound, his soul crawled back painfully, through subterranean corridors, up into his body again. Toward the last it moved to a cacophony of hammers and lights.

Then he was awake.

The first eye was bad enough. But, when he opened the second eye, such a rush of anguish flowed through his brain that he hastily closed them again.

He observed – at first without curiosity – that he was lying in bed in a room he had never seen before; that he wore pajamas; and that there was sunlight in the room.

But his original concerns were purely physical. His head felt as though it were rising toward the ceiling with long, spiraling motions; his stomach was an inferno, his voice a croak out of a dry throat, his whole being composed of fine wriggling wires. Thus Alan Campbell, waking at twelve midday with the king of all hangovers, for the moment merely lay and suffered.

Presently he tried to climb out of bed. But dizziness overcame him, and he lay down again. It was here that his wits began to work, however. Feverishly he tried to remember what had happened last night.

And he could not remember a single thing.

Alan was galvanized.

Possible enormities stretched out behind him, whole vistas of enormities which he might have said or done, but which he could not remember now. There is perhaps not in the world any anguish to compare to this. He knew, or presumed, that he was still at the Castle of Shira; and that he had been lured into quaffing the Doom of the Campbells with Colin; but this was all he knew.

The door of the room opened, and Kathryn came in.

On a tray she carried a cup of black coffee and a revolting-looking mixture in a glass eggcup. She was fully dressed. But the wan expression on her face and eyes strangely comforted him.

Kathryn came over and put down the tray on the bedside table.

"Well, Dr Campbell," were her first unencouraging words, "don't you feel ashamed of yourself?"

All Alan's emotion found vent in one lingering passionate groan.

"Heaven knows *I've* no right to blame you," said Kathryn, putting her hands to her head. "I was almost as bad as you were. Oh, God, I feel *awful!*" she breathed, and tottered on her feet. "But at least I didn't –"

"Didn't what?" croaked Alan.

"Don't you remember?"

He waited for enormity to sweep him like the sea.

"At the moment – no. Nothing."

She pointed to the tray. "Drink that prairie oyster. I know it looks foul; but it'll do you good."

"No: tell me. What did I do? Was I very bad?"

Kathryn eyed him wanly.

"Not as bad as Colin, of course. But when *I* tried to leave the party, you and Colin were fencing with claymores."

"Were what?"

"Fencing with real swords. All over the dining-room and out in the hall and up the stairs. You had kitchen tablecloths slung on for plaids. Colin was talking in Gaelic, and you were quoting *Marmion*, and *The Lady of the Lake*. Only you couldn't seem to decide whether you were Roderick Dhu or Douglas Fairbanks."

Alan shut his eyes tightly.

He breathed a prayer himself. Faint glimmers, like chinks of light in a blind, touched old-world scenes which swam at him and then receded in hopeless confusion. All lights splintered; all voices dimmed.

"Stop a bit!" he said, pressing his hands to his forehead. "There's nothing about Elspat in this, is there? I didn't insult Elspat, did I? I seem to remember . . ."

Again he shut his eyes.

"My dear Alan, that's the one good feature of the whole night. You're Aunt Elspat's white-haired boy. She thinks that you, next to the late Angus, are the finest member of the whole family."

"What?"

"Don't you remember giving her a lecture at least half an hour long, about the Solemn League and Covenant and the history of the Church of Scotland?"

"Wait! I do seem vaguely to –"

"She didn't understand it; but you had her spellbound. She said that anybody who knew the names of so many ministers couldn't be as godless as she'd thought. Then you insisted on her having half a tumbler of that wretched stuff, and she walked off to bed like Lady Macbeth. This was before the fencing episode, of course. And then – don't you remember what Colin did to that poor man Swan?"

"Swan? Not the MacHolster Swan?"

"Yes."

"But what was *he* doing here?"

"Well, it was something like this: though it's rather dim in my own mind. After you'd fenced all over the place, Colin wanted to go out. He said, 'Alan Oig, there is dirty work to be done this night. Let us hence and look for Stewarts.' You thought that would be a perfectly splendid idea.

"We went out the back, on the road. The first thing we saw, in the bright moonlight, was Mr Swan standing and looking at the house. Don't ask me what he was doing there! Colin whooped out, 'There's a bluidy Stewart!' and went for him with the claymore.

"Mr Swan took one look at him, and shot off down the road harder than I've ever seen any man run before. Colin went tearing after him, and you after Colin. I didn't interfere. I'd reached the stage where all I could do was stand and giggle. Colin couldn't quite manage to overtake Mr Swan, but he did manage to stick him several times in the – in the –"

"Yes."

"– before Colin fell flat and Mr Swan got away. Then you two came back singing."

There was obviously something on Kathryn's mind. She kept her eyes on the floor.

"I suppose you don't remember," she added, "that I spent the night in here?"

"*You spent the night in here?*"

"Yes. Colin wouldn't hear of anything else. He locked us in."

"But we didn't . . . I mean . . . ?"

"Didn't what?"

"You know what I mean."

Kathryn evidently did, to judge by her color.

"Well – no. We were both too far gone, anyway. I was so dizzy and weak that I didn't even protest. You recited something about,

> 'Here dies in my bosom
> The secret of heather ale.'

"Then you courteously said, 'Excuse me,' and lay down on the floor and went to sleep."

He became conscious of his pajamas. "But how did I get into these?"

"I don't know. You must have woken up in the night and put them on. I woke up about six o'clock, feeling like death, and managed to push the key in the door out, so it fell on the outside and I dragged it under the sill on a piece of paper. I got off to my own room, and I don't think Elspat knows anything about it. But when I woke up and found you there . . ."

Her voice rose almost to a wail.

"Alan Campbell, what on earth has come over us? Both of us? Don't you think we'd better get out of Scotland before it corrupts us altogether?"

Alan reached out for the prairie oyster. How he managed to swallow it he does not now remember; but he did, and felt better. The hot black coffee helped.

"So help me," he declared, "I will never touch another drop as long as I live! And Colin. I hope he's suffering the tortures of the inferno. I hope he's got such a hangover as will –"

"Well, he hasn't."

"No?"

"He's as bright as a cricket. He says good whisky never gave any man a headache. That dreadful Dr Fell has arrived, too. Can you come downstairs and get some breakfast?"

Alan gritted his teeth.

"I'll have a try," he said, "if you can overcome your lack of decency and get out of here while I dress."

Half an hour later, after shaving and bathing in the somewhat primitive bathroom, he was on his way downstairs feeling much better. From the partly open door of the sitting-room came the sound of two powerful voices, those of Colin and Dr Fell, which sent sharp pains through his skull. Toast was all he could manage in the way of breakfast. Afterwards he and Kathryn crept guiltily into the sitting-room.

Dr Fell, his hand folded over his crutch-handled stick, sat on the sofa. The broad black ribbon of his eyeglasses blew out as he chuckled. His big mop of gray-streaked hair lay over one eye, and many more chins appeared as his amusement increased. He seemed to fill the room: at first Alan could hardly believe him.

"Good morning!" he thundered.

"Good morning!" thundered Colin.

"Good morning," murmured Alan. "Must you shout like that?"

"Nonsense. We weren't shouting," said Colin. "How are you feeling this morning?"

"Terrible."

Colin stared at him. "You haven't got a head?"

"No?"

"Nonsense!" snorted Colin, fiercely and dogmatically. "Good whisky never gave any man a head."

This fallacy, by the way, is held almost as a gospel in the North. Alan did not attempt to dispute it. Dr Fell hoisted himself ponderously to his feet and made something in the nature of a bow.

"Your servant, sir," said Dr Fell. He bowed to Kathryn. "And yours, madam." A twinkle appeared in his eye. "I trust that you have now managed to settle between you the vexed question of the Duchess of Cleveland's hair? Or may I infer that at the moment you are more interested in the hair of the dog?"

"That's not a bad idea, you know," said Colin.

"No!" roared Alan, and made his own head ache. "I will never touch that damned stuff again under any circumstances. That is final."

"That's what you think now," Colin grinned comfortably. "I'm going to give Fell here a nip of it tonight. I say, my boy: would you like to taste some mountain dew that'll take the top of your head off?"

Dr Fell chuckled.

"It would be very interesting," he replied, "to find any whisky that could take the top of my head off."

"Don't say that," warned Alan. "Let me urge you in advance: don't say it. *I* said it. It's fatal."

"And must we talk about this, anyway?" inquired Kathryn, who had been eyeing Dr Fell with a deep suspicion which he returned by beaming like the Ghost of Christmas Present.

Rather to their surprise, Dr Fell grew grave.

"Oddly enough, I think it would be advisable to talk of it. Archons of Athens! It's quite possible the matter may have some bearing on –"

He hesitated.

"On what?"

"On Angus Campbell's murder," said Dr Fell.

Colin whistled, and then there was a silence. Muttering to himself, Dr Fell appeared to be trying to chew at the end of his bandit's mustache.

"Perhaps," he went on, "I had better explain. I was very happy to get my friend Colin Campbell's invitation. I was much intrigued by the full details of the case as he wrote them. Putting in my pocket my *Boswell* and my toothbrush, I took a train for the North. I beguiled my time rereading the great Doctor Johnson's views on this country. You are no doubt familiar with his stern reply when told that he should not be so hard on Scotland since, after all, God had made Scotland? 'Sir, comparisons are invidious; but God made hell.'"

Colin gestured impatiently. "Never mind that. What were you saying?"

"I arrived in Dunoon," said Dr Fell, "early yesterday evening. I tried to get a car at the tourist agency –"

"We know it," said Kathryn.

"But was informed that the only car then available had already taken a batch of people to Shira. I asked when the car would be back. The clerk said it would not be back. He said he had just that moment received a telephone call from Inveraray from the driver, a man named Fleming –"

"Jock," Colin explained to the others.

"The driver said that one of his passengers, a gentleman called Swan, had decided to stay the night in Inveraray, and wanted to keep car and driver to take him back to Dunoon in the morning. This, with suitable costs, was arranged."

"Infernal snooper," roared Colin.

"One moment. The clerk said, however, that if I would come to the agency at half past nine in the morning – this morning – the car would be back and would take me to Shira.

"I spent the night at the hotel, and was there on time. I then observed the somewhat unusual spectacle of a motorcar coming along the main street with its one passenger, a man in a gray hat and a very violent tartan necktie, standing up in the back seat."

Colin Campbell glowered at the floor.

A vast, dreamy expression of pleasure went over Dr Fell's face. His eye was on a corner of the ceiling. He cleared his throat.

"Intrigued as to why this man should be standing up, I made inquiries. He replied (somewhat curtly) that he found the sitting position painful. It required little subtlety to get the story out of him. Indeed, he was boiling with it. Harrumph."

Alan groaned.

Dr Fell peered over his eyeglasses, first at Alan and then at Kathryn. He wheezed. His expression was one of gargantuan delicacy.

"May I inquire," he said, "whether you two are engaged to be married?"

"Certainly not!" cried Kathryn.

"Then," Dr Fell urged warmly, "in heaven's name *get* married. Do it in a hurry. You both hold responsible positions. But what you are likely to read about yourselves in today's *Daily Floodlight*, at risk of libel or no, is not likely to find favor with either Highgate University or the Harpenden College for Women. That thrilling story of the moonlight chase with claymores, with the lady shouting encouragement while the two cutthroats pursued him, really did put the tin hat on it."

"I never shouted encouragement!" said Kathryn.

Dr Fell blinked at her.

"Are you sure you didn't, ma'am?"

"Well . . ."

"I'm afraid you did, Kitty-kat," observed Colin, glaring at the floor. "But it was my fault. I –"

Dr Fell made a gesture.

"No matter," he said. "That was not what I wanted to tell you. Intrigued and inspired by this revival of old Highland customs, I spoke with the driver, Mr Fleming."

"Yes?"

"Now here is what I most seriously want to ask. Did any of you, last night, at any time go up into the tower? *Any of you, at any time?*"

There was a silence. The windows facing the loch were open to a clear, cool, pleasant day. They all looked at each other.

"No," returned Kathryn.

"No," stated Colin.

"You're quite sure of that, now?"

"Definitely."

"Mr Swan," Dr Fell went on, with a curious insistence which Alan found disturbing, "says that the two men were 'dressed up' in some way."

"Oh, it's silly and horrible!" said Kathryn. "And it's all Alan's fault. They weren't exactly 'dressed up.' They had checkered tablecloths draped over their shoulders for plaids, that's all."

"Nothing else?"

"No."

Dr Fell drew in his breath. His expression remained so grave, his color so high, that nobody spoke.

"I repeat," Dr Fell continued, "that I questioned the driver. Getting information out of him was rather more difficult than drawing teeth. But on one point he did give some information. He says that this place is not 'canny' –"

Colin interrupted with a fierce grunt of impatience, but Dr Fell silenced him.

"And now he says he's in a position to swear to it."

"How?"

"Last night, after they had put up at Inveraray, Swan asked him to drive back here. Swan was going to have another try at getting in to see Miss Elspat Campbell. Now let's see if I've got the geography straight. The road to Inveraray runs along the back of the house, doesn't it?"

"Yes."

"And the front door faces the loch, as we see. Swan asked the driver to walk round and knock at the front door, as a sort of messenger, while Swan remained at the back. The driver did so. It was bright moonlight, remember."

"Well?"

"He was just about to knock at the door, when he happened to look up at the window of the tower room. And he saw somebody or something at that window."

"But that's impossible!" cried Kathryn. "We were –"

Dr Fell examined his hands, which were folded on the handle of his stick.

Then Dr Fell looked up.

"Fleming," he went on, "swears he saw something in Highland costume, with half its face shot away, looking down at him."

10

It is all very well to be hard headed. Most of us are, even with headaches and shaky nerves. But to find a breath of superstitious terror is far from difficult here.

"Were you thinking," asked Kathryn, "of that story of what happened after the massacre of Glencoe? That the ghost of one of the victims pursued a man called Ian Campbell, who –"

Despairing of words, she made a gesture as of one who jumps.

Colin's face was fiery.

"Ghosts!" he said. "Ghosts! Look here. In the first place, there never was any such tradition as that. It was put into a lying guide-book because it sounded pretty. Professional soldiers in those days weren't so thin-skinned about executing orders.

"In the second place, that room's not haunted. Angus slept there every night for years, and *he* never saw a bogle. You don't believe such rubbish, do you, Fell?"

Dr Fell remained unruffled.

"I am merely," he answered mildly, "stating what the driver told me."

"Rubbish. Jock was pulling your leg."

"And yet, d'ye know" – Dr Fell screwed up his face – "he

hardly struck me as a man addicted to that form of gammon. I have usually found that Gaels will joke about anything except ghosts. Besides, I think you miss the real point of the story."

He was silent for a moment.

"But when did this happen?" asked Alan.

"Ah, yes. It was just before the two cut-throats with their lady came out of the back door and set on Swan. Fleming didn't knock at the front door after all. Hearing the shouts, he went to the back. He started up his car and eventually picked up Swan on the road. But he says he wasn't feeling too well. He says he stood in the moonlight for several minutes after he'd seen the thing at the window, and didn't feel too well at all. I can't say I blame him."

Kathryn hesitated. "What did it look like?"

"Bonnet and plaid and face caved in. That's all he could tell with any distinctness."

"Not a kilt too?"

"He wouldn't have been able to see a kilt. He only saw the upper half of the figure. He says it looked decayed, as though the moths had got at it, and it had only one eye." Again the doctor cleared his throat, rumblingly. "The point, however, is this. Who, besides you three, was in the house last night?"

"Nobody," replied Kathryn, "except Aunt Elspat and Kirstie, the maid. And they'd gone to bed."

"I tell you it's rubbish!" snarled Colin.

"Well, you can speak to Jock himself if you like. He's out in the kitchen now."

Colin rose to find Jock and end this nonsense; but he did not do so. Alistair Duncan, followed by a patient but weary-looking Walter Chapman, was ushered in by the maid Kirstie – a scared-eyed, soft-voiced girl whose self-effacing habits rendered her almost invisible.

The lawyer made no reference to last night's rumpus with Colin. He stood very stiffly.

"Colin Campbell –" he began.

"Look here," grumbled Colin, shoving his hands into his pockets, lowering his neck into his collar, and looking like a Newfoundland dog which has been at the larder. "I owe you an apology, dammit. I apologize. I was wrong. There."

Duncan expelled his breath.

"I am glad, sir, that you have the decency to acknowledge it. Only my long friendship with your family enables me to overlook a piece of ill manners so uncalled for and so flagrant."

"Hoy! Now wait a bit! Wait a bit! I didn't say –"

"So let us think no more about it," concluded the lawyer, as Colin's eye began to gleam again. Duncan coughed, indicating that he had left personal matters and now dealt with business.

"I thought I had better inform you," he went on, "that they think they may have found Alec Forbes."

"Wow! Where?"

"He's been reported to have been seen at a crofter's cottage near Glencoe."

Chapman intervened.

"Can't we settle it?" the insurance man suggested. "Glencoe's no great distance from here, as I understand it. You could drive there and back easily in an afternoon. Why not hop in my car and run up and see him?"

The lawyer's manner had a sort of corpse-like benevolence.

"Patience, my dear fellow. Patience, patience, patience! First let the police find out if it *is* Alec. He has been reported before, you remember. Once in Edinburgh and once in Ayr."

"Alec Forbes," struck in Dr Fell, "being the sinister figure who called on Mr Campbell the night the latter died?"

They all swung round. Colin hastily performed an introduction.

"I have heard of you, Doctor," said Duncan, scrutinizing Dr Fell through his pince-nez. "In fact, I – ah – confess I came here partly in the hope of seeing you. We have here, of course," he smiled, "a clear case of murder. But we are still rather confused about it. Can you unriddle it for us?"

For a moment Dr Fell did not reply.

He frowned at the floor, drawing a design on the carpet with the end of his stick.

"H'mf," he said, and gave the ferrule of the stick a rap on the floor. "I sincerely trust it is murder. If it is not, I have no interest in it. But – Alec Forbes! Alec Forbes! Alec Forbes!"

"What about him?"

"Well, who is Alec Forbes? What is he? I could bear to know much more of him. For instance: what was the cause of his quarrel with Mr Campbell?"

"Ice-cream," replied Colin.

"What?"

"Ice-cream. They were going to make it by a new process, in great quantity. And it was to be colored in different tartan patterns. No, I'm perfectly serious! That's the sort of idea Angus was always getting. They built a laboratory, and used artificial ice – that chemical stuff that's so expensive – and ran up bills and raised merry blazes. Another of Angus's ideas was a new kind of tractor that would both sow and reap. And he also financed those people who were going to find Drake's gold and make all the subscribers millionaires."

"What sort of person is Forbes? Laboring man? Something of that sort?"

"Oh, no. Bloke of some education. But scatty in the money line, like Angus. Lean, dark-faced chap. Moody. Fond of the bottle. Great cyclist."

"H'mf. I see." Dr Fell pointed with his stick. "That's Angus Campbell's photograph on the mantelpiece there, I take it?"

"Yes."

Dr Fell got up from the sofa and lumbered across. He carried the crepe-draped picture to the light, adjusted his eyeglasses, and puffed gently as he studied it.

"Not the face, you know," he said, "of a man who commits suicide."

"Definitely not," smiled the lawyer.

"But we can't –" Chapman began.

"Which Campbell are you, sir?" Dr Fell asked politely.

Chapman threw up his arms in despair.

"I'm not a Campbell at all. I represent the Hercules Insurance Company and I've got to get back to my office in Glasgow or business will go to blazes. See here, Dr Fell. I've heard of you too. They say you're fair-minded. And I put it to you: how can we go by what a person 'would' or 'wouldn't' have done, when the evidence shows he *did* do it?"

"All evidence," said Dr Fell, "points two ways. Like the ends of a stick. That is the trouble with it."

Absentmindedly he stumped back to the mantelpiece, and put the photograph down. He seemed very much disturbed. While his eyeglasses came askew on his nose, he made what was (for him) the great exertion of feeling through all his pockets. He produced a sheet of paper scrawled with notes.

"From the admirably clear letter written by Colin Campbell," he went on, "and from facts he has given me this morning, I have been trying to construct a précis of what we know, or think we know."

"Well?" prompted the lawyer.

"With your permission" – Dr Fell scowled hideously – "I should like to read out these points. One or two things may appear a little clearer, or at least more suggestive, if they are heard in skeleton form. Correct me if I am wrong in any of them.

"1. Angus Campbell always went to bed at ten o'clock.

"2. It was his habit to lock and bolt the door on the inside.

"3. It was his habit to sleep with the window shut.

"4. It was his habit to write up his diary each night before going to bed."

Dr Fell blinked up.

"No misstatement there, I trust?"

"No," admitted Colin.

"Then we pass on to the simple circumstances surrounding the crime.

"5. Alec Forbes called on A. Campbell at nine-thirty on the night of the crime.

"6. He forced his way into the house, and went up to Angus's bedroom.

"7. Neither of the two women saw him at this time."

Dr Fell rubbed his nose.

"Query," he added, "how did Forbes get in, then? Presumably he didn't just break down the front door?"

"If you'd like to step out of that door there," responded Colin, pointing, "you can see. It leads to the ground floor of the tower. In the ground-floor room there are wooden double-doors leading out to the court. They're supposed to be padlocked, but half the time they're not. That's how Forbes came – without disturbing anybody else."

Dr Fell made a note.

"That seems to be clear enough. Very well. We now take arms against a sea of troubles.

"8. At this time Forbes was carrying an object like a 'suitcase.'

"9. He had a row with Angus, who evicted him.

"10. Forbes was empty-handed when he left.

"11. Elspat Campbell and Kirstie MacTavish arrived in time to see the eviction.

"12. They were afraid Forbes might have come back. This becomes more understandable when we learn of the isolated tower with its outside entrance and its five empty floors.

"13. They searched the empty room, and also Angus's room.

"14. There was nothing under the bed in Angus's bedroom at
this time.

"Still correct?" inquired Dr Fell, raising his head.

"No, it isna," announced a high, sharp, positive voice which
made them all jump.

Nobody had seen Aunt Elspat come in. She stood sternly on
her dignity, her hands folded.

Dr Fell blinked at her. "What isn't true, ma'am?"

"It isna true tae say the box tae carry the dog wasna under the
bed when Kirstie and I luked. It was."

Her six auditors regarded her with consternation. Most of
them began to speak at once, frantic babble which was only
stilled by Duncan's stern assertion of legal authority.

"Elspat Campbell, listen to me. You said there was nothing
there."

"I said there was nae *suitcase* there. I didna say aboot the ither
thing."

"Are you telling us that the dog carrier was under the bed
before Angus locked and bolted his door?"

"Aye."

"Elspat," said Colin, with a sudden gleam of certainty in his
eye, "you're lying. God's wounds, you're lying! You said there
was *nothing* under that bed. I heard you myself."

"I'm tellin' ye the gospel truth, and Kirstie will tu." She
favored them all with an equally malignant look. "Dinner's on
its way, and I'm no' settin' places for the parcel o' ye."

Inflexible, making this very clear, she walked out of the room
and closed the door.

The question is, thought Alan, does this alter matters or
doesn't it? He shared Colin Campbell's evident conviction that
Elspat was lying. But she had one of those faces so used to
household deceit, so experienced in lying for what she believed

a good purpose, that it was difficult to distinguish between truth and falsehood in anything.

This time it was Dr Fell who stilled the babble of argument.

"We will query the point," he said, "and continue. The next points define our problem squarely and simply.

"15. Angus locked and bolted his door on the inside.
"16. His dead body was found by the milkman at six o'clock on the following morning, at the foot of the tower.
"17. He had died of multiple injuries caused by the fall.
"18. Death took place between ten p.m. and one a.m.
"19. He had not been drugged or overcome in any way.
"20. The door was still locked and bolted on the inside. Since the bolt was rusty, difficult to draw and firmly shot in its socket, this rules out any possibility of tampering with it."

In Alan's mind rose the image of the shattered door as he had seen it last night.

He remembered the rustiness of the bolt, and the stubborn lock torn from its frame. Jiggery-pokery with string or any similar device must clearly be put aside. The image faded as Dr Fell continued.

"21. The window was inaccessible. We have this from a steeplejack.
"22. There was no person hiding in the room.
"23. The bed had been occupied."

Dr Fell puffed out his cheeks, frowned, and tapped a pencil on the notes.

"Which," he said, "brings us to a point where I must interpose another query. Your letter didn't say. When his body was found in the morning, was he wearing slippers or a dressing gown?"

"No," said Colin. "Just his wool nightshirt."

Dr Fell made another note.

"24. His diary was missing. This, however, might have been taken at some subsequent time.

"25. Angus's fingerprints, and only his, were found on the catch of the window.

"26. Under the bed was a case of the sort used to carry dogs. It did not belong in the house; had presumably been brought by Forbes; but was in any case not there the night before.

"27. This box was empty.

"We are therefore forced to the conclusion –"

Dr Fell paused.

"Go on!" Alistair Duncan prompted in a sharp voice. "To what conclusion?"

Dr Fell sniffed.

"Gentlemen, we can't escape it. It's inevitable. We are forced to the conclusion that either (a) Angus Campbell deliberately committed suicide, or (b) there was in that box something which made him run for his life to escape it, and crash through the window to his death in doing so."

Kathryn shivered a little. But Chapman was not impressed.

"I know," he said. "Snakes, spiders. Fu Manchu. We were all over that last night. And it gets us nowhere."

"Can you dispute my facts?" inquired Dr Fell, taping the notes.

"No. But can you dispute *mine*? Snakes! Spiders –"

"And now," grinned Colin, "ghosts."

"Eh?"

"A *rattlebrain* by the name of Jock Fleming," explained Colin, "claims to have seen somebody in Highland dress, with no face, gibbering at the window last night."

Chapman's face lost some of its color.

"I don't know anything about that," he said. "But I could almost as soon believe in a ghost as in a dexterous spider or snake that could close up the clasps of a suitcase afterwards. I'm English. I'm practical. But this is a funny country and a funny house; and I tell you *I* shouldn't care to spend a night up in that room."

Colin got up from his chair and did a little dance round the room.

"That's done it," he roared, when he could get his breath. *"That's torn it!"*

Dr Fell blinked at him with mild expostulation. Colin's face was suffused and the veins stood out on his thick neck.

"Listen," he went on, swallowing with powerful restraint. "Ever since I got here, everybody has been ghosting me. And I'm sick of it. This tomfoolery has got to be blown sky-high and I'm the jasper to do it. I'll tell you what I'm going to do. I'm going to move my things into that tower this very afternoon, and I'm going to sleep there henceforward. If so much as a ghost of a ghost shows its ugly head there, if anybody tries to make *me* jump out of a window . . ."

His eye fell on the family Bible. The atheistical Colin ran across to it and put his hand on it.

"Then I hereby swear that I'll go to the kirk every Sunday for the next twelve months. Yes, and prayer-meeting too!"

He darted across to the door to the hall, which he set open.

"Do you hear that, Elspat?" he roared, coming back and putting his hand on the Bible again. "Every Sunday, and prayer-meeting on Wednesdays. Ghosts! Bogles! Warlocks! Isn't there a sane person left in this world?"

His voice reverberated through the house. You might have imagined that it drew back echoes. But Kathryn's attempt to shush him was unnecessary. Colin already felt better. It was Kirstie MacTavish who supplied the distraction, by thrusting her head in at the doorway and speaking in a tone not far removed from real awe.

"That reporter's back again," she said.

11

Colin opened his eyes. "Not the chap from the *Daily Floodlight*?"

"It's him."

"Tell him I'll see him," said Colin, straightening his collar and drawing a deep breath.

"No!" said Alan. "In your present state of mind you'd probably cut his heart out and eat it. Let *me* see him."

"Yes, please!" cried Kathryn. She turned a fervent face. "If he's dared to come back here, he can't have said anything very awful about us in the paper. Don't you see: this is our chance to apologize and put everything right again? Please let Alan see him!"

"All right," Colin agreed. "After all, you didn't stick him in the seat of his pants with a claymore. You may be able to smooth him down."

Alan hurried out into the hall. Just outside the front door, clearly of two minds on how to approach this interview, stood Swan. Alan went outside, and carefully closed the front door.

"Look here," he began, "I honestly am terribly sorry about last night. I can't think what came over us. We'd had one over the eight . . ."

"You're telling *me*?" inquired Swan. He looked at Alan, and anger seemed less predominant than real curiosity. "What were you drinking, for God's sake? TNT and monkey glands? I used to be a track man myself, but I never saw anybody cover ground like that thick-set old buster since Nurmi retired to Finland."

"Something like that."

Swan's expression, as he saw that he was dealing with a chastened man, grew increasingly more stern.

"Now look," he said impressively. "You know, don't you, that I could sue you all for heavy damages?"

"Yes, but –"

"And that I've got enough on you to make your name mud in the Press, if I was the sort of a fellow who bears malice?"

"Yes, but –"

"You can just thank your lucky stars, Dr Campbell, that I'm *not* the sort of fellow who bears malice: that's all I say." Swan gave a significant nod. He was wearing a new light-gray suit and tartan tie. Again his gloomy sternness was moved by curiosity. "What kind of a professor are you anyway? Running around with women professors from other colleges – always going to houses of ill fame –"

"Here! For the love of –"

"Now don't deny it," said Swan, pointing a lean finger in his face. "I heard Miss Campbell herself say, in front of witnesses, that that's exactly what you were always doing."

"She was talking about the Roman Catholic Church! That's what the old-timers called it."

"It's not what the old-timers called it where *I* come from. On top of that, you get all ginned up and chase respectable people along a public road with broadswords. Do you carry on like that at Highgate, Doc? Or just in vacations? I really want to know."

"I swear to you, it's all a mistake! And here's the point. I don't care what you say about me. But will you promise not to say anything about Miss Campbell?"

Swan considered this.

"Well, I don't know," he said, with another darkly significant shake of his head, and a suggestion that, if he did this, it would be only from the kindness of his heart. "I've got a duty to the public, you know."

"Rubbish."

"But I'll tell you what I'll do," Swan suggested, as though suddenly coming to a decision. "Just to show you I'm a sport, I'll make a deal with you."

"Deal?"

The other lowered his voice.

"That fellow in there, the great big fat fellow, is Dr Gideon Fell: isn't it?"

"Yes."

"I only discovered it when he'd slipped away from me. And, when I phoned my paper, they were pretty wild. They say that wherever *he* goes, a story breaks with a wallop. They say to stick to him. Look, Doc. I've *got* to get a story! I've incurred a lot of expense over this thing; I've got another car that's eating its head off. If I fall down on this story I won't get the expenses OK'd, and I may even get the air."

"So?"

"So here's what I want you to do. Just keep me posted, that's all. Let me know everything that goes on. In return for that —"

He paused, shying back a little, as Colin Campbell came out of the front door. But Colin was trying to be affable, too affable, massively affable, with a guilty grin.

"In return for that, just keeping me posted," resumed Swan, "I'll agree to forget all I know about you and Miss Campbell, *and*" — he looked at Colin — "what you did as well, which might have caused me a serious injury. I'll do that just to be a sport and show there are no hard feelings. What do you say?"

Colin's face had lightened with relief.

"I say it's fair enough," Colin returned, with a bellow of pleasure. "Now that's damned decent of you, young fellow! Damned decent! I was tight and I apologize. What do you say, Alan Oig?"

Alan's voice was fervent.

"I say it's fair enough too. You keep to that bargain, Mr Swan, and you'll have nothing to complain about. If there are any stories going, you shall have them."

He could almost forget that he had a hangover. A beautiful sense of well-being, a sense of the world set right again, crept into Alan Campbell and glowed in his veins.

Swan raised his eyebrows.

"Then it's a deal?"

"It is," said Colin.

"It is," agreed the other miscreant.

"All right, then!" said Swan, drawing a deep breath but still speaking darkly. "Only just remember that I'm straining my duty to my public to oblige you. So remember where we all stand and don't try any –"

Above their heads, a window creaked open. The contents of a large bucket of water, aimed with deadly and scientific accuracy, descended in a solid, glistening sheet over Swan's head. In fact, Swan might be said momentarily to have disappeared.

At the window appeared the malignant face of Aunt Elspat.

"Can ye no' tak' a hint?" she inquired. "I tauld ye to gang your ways, and I'll no' tell ye again. Here's for guid measure."

With the same accuracy, but almost with leisureliness, she lifted a second bucket and emptied it over Swan's head. Then the window closed with a bang.

Swan did not say anything. He stood motionless, and merely looked. His new suit was slowly turning black. His hat resembled a piece of sodden blotting paper from beneath whose down-turned brim there looked out the eyes of a man gradually being bereft of his reason.

"My dear chap!" bellowed Colin in real consternation. "The old witch! I'll wring her neck; so help me, I will! My dear chap, you're not hurt, are you?"

Colin bounded down the steps. Swan began slowly, but with increasing haste, to back away from him.

"My dear chap, wait! Stop! You must have some dry clothes!"

Swan continued to back away.

"Come into the house, my dear fellow. Come –"

Then Swan found his voice.

"Come into the house," he shrilled, backing away still farther, "so you can steal my clothes and turn me out again? No, you don't! Keep away from me!"

"Look out!" screamed Colin. "One more step and you'll be in the loch! Look –"

Alan glanced round wildly. At the windows of the sitting-room observed an interested group of watchers composed of Duncan, Chapman, and Dr Fell. But most of all he was conscious of Kathryn's horror-stricken countenance.

Swan saved himself by some miracle on the edge of the pier.

"Think I'll go into that booby-hatch, do you?" Swan was raving. "You're a bunch of criminal lunatics, that's what you are, and I'm going to expose you. I'm going to –"

"Man, you can't walk about like that! You'll catch your death of cold! Come on in. Besides," argued Colin, "you'll be on the scene of it, won't you? Smack in the middle of things alongside Dr Fell?"

This appeared to make Swan pause. He hesitated. Still streaming like an enthusiastic fountain, he wiped the water from his eyes with a shaky hand, and looked back at Colin with real entreaty.

"Can I depend on that?"

"I swear you can! The old hag has got it in for you, but I'll take care of her. Come on."

Swan seemed to be debating courses. At length he allowed himself to be taken by the arm and urged toward the door. He ducked quickly when he passed the window, as though wondering whether to expect boiling lead.

A scene of some embarrassment ensued inside. The lawyer and the insurance man took a hasty leave. Colin, clucking to his charge, escorted him upstairs to change his clothes. In the sitting-room a dejected Alan found Kathryn and Dr Fell.

"I trust, sir," observed Dr Fell, with stately courtesy, "you know your own business best. But, candidly, do you really think it's wise to antagonize the press quite so much at that? What did you do to the fellow this time? Duck him in the water butt?"

"We didn't do anything. It was Elspat. She poured two buckets of water on him from the window."

"But is he going to –?" cried Kathryn.

"He promises that if we keep him posted about what's going on here, he won't say a word. At least, that's what he *did* promise. I can't say how he's feeling now."

"Keep him posted?" asked Dr Fell sharply.

"Presumably about what's going on here, and whether this is suicide or murder, and what you think of it." Alan paused. "What do you think, by the way?"

Dr Fell's gaze moved to the door to the hall, making sure it was firmly closed. He puffed out his cheeks, shook his head, and finally sat down on the sofa again.

"If only the facts," he growled, "weren't so infernally simple! I distrust their simplicity. I have a feeling that there's a trap in them. I should also like to know why Miss Elspat Campbell now wants to change her testimony, and swears that the dog carrier *was* under the bed before the room was locked up."

"Do you think the second version is true?"

"No, by thunder, I don't!" said Dr Fell, rapping his stick on the floor. "I think the first is true. But that only makes our locked-room problem the worse. Unless –"

"Unless what?"

Dr Fell disregarded this.

"It apparently does no good merely to repeat those twenty-seven points over and over. I repeat: it's too simple. A man double-locks his door. He goes to bed. He gets up in the middle of the night without his slippers (mark that), and jumps from the window to instant death. He –"

"That's not quite accurate, by the way."

Dr Fell lifted his head, his under-lip out-thrust.

"Hey? What isn't?"

"Well, if you insist on a shade of accuracy, Angus didn't meet an instant death. At least, so Colin told me. The police surgeon wouldn't be definite about the time of death. He said Angus hadn't died instantly, but had probably been alive though unconscious for a little while before he died."

Dr Fell's little eyes narrowed. The wheezing breaths, which ran down over the ridges of his waistcoat, were almost stilled. He seemed about to say something, but checked himself.

"I further," he said, "don't like Colin's insistence on spending the night in that tower room."

"You don't think there's any more danger?" Kathryn asked.

"My dear child! Of course there's danger!" said Dr Fell. "There's always danger when some agency we don't understand killed a man. Pry the secret out of it, and you're all right. But so long as you don't understand it . . ."

He brooded.

"You have probably observed that the very things we try hardest to avoid happening are always the things that do happen. *Vide* the saga of Swan. But here, in an uglier way, we have the same wheel revolving and the same danger returning. Archons of Athens! What COULD have been in that dog carrier? Something that left *no* trace, nothing whatever? And why the open end? Obviously so that something could breathe through the wire and get air. But what?"

Distorted pictures, all without form, floated in Alan's mind.

"You don't think the box may be a red herring?"

"It may be. But, unless it does mean something, the whole case collapses and we may as well go home to bed. It has got to mean something."

"Some kind of animal?" suggested Kathryn.

"Which closed the clasps of the box after it got out?" inquired Dr Fell.

"That may not be so difficult," Alan pointed out, "if it were thin enough to get out through the wire. No, hang it, that won't do!" He remembered the box itself, and the mesh. "That wire is so close-meshed that the smallest snake in existence could hardly wriggle out through it."

"Then," pursued Dr Fell, "there is the episode of the Highlander with the caved-in face."

"You don't believe that story?"

"I believe that Jock Fleming saw what he says he saw. I do not necessarily believe in a ghost. After all, such a piece of trickery, in the moonlight and from a distance of sixty feet up in a tower, wouldn't be very difficult. An old bonnet and plaid, a little makeup –"

"But why?"

Dr Fell's eyes opened wide. His breath labored with ghoulish eagerness as he seemed to seize on the point.

"Exactly. That's it. Why? We mustn't miss the importance of the tale: which is not whether it was supernatural, but why it was done at all. That is, if it had any reason at all in the way we mean." He became very thoughtful. "Find the contents of that box, and we're on the view-halloo. That's our problem. Some parts of the business, of course, are easy. You will already have guessed who stole the missing diary?"

"Of course," replied Kathryn instantly. "*Elspat* stole it, of course."

Alan stared at her.

Dr Fell, with a vast and gratified beam, regarded her as though she were a more refreshing person than even he had expected, and nodded.

"Admirable!" he chuckled. "The talent for deduction developed by judicious historical research can just as well be applied to detective work. Never forget that, my dear. *I* learned it at an early age. Bull's-eye. It was Elspat for a fiver."

"But why?" demanded Alan.

Kathryn set her face into its severest lines, as though they had again returned to the debate of two nights ago. Her tone was withering.

"My *dear* Dr Campbell!" she said. "Consider what we know. For many, many years she was rather more than a housekeeper to Angus Campbell?"

"Well?"

"But she's horribly, morbidly respectable, and doesn't even believe anybody's guessed her real thoughts?"

(Alan was tempted to say, "Something like you," but he restrained himself.)

"Yes."

"Angus Campbell was a free-spoken person who kept a diary where he could record his intimate – well, you know!"

"Yes?"

"All right. Three days before his death, Angus takes out still another insurance policy, to take care of his old-time love in the event of his death. It's almost certain, isn't it, that in writing down that he did take out an insurance policy he'll make some reference to *why* he did it?"

She paused, raising her eyebrows.

"So, of course, Elspat stole the diary out of some horrid fear of having people learn what she did years and years ago.

"Don't you remember what happened last night, Alan? How she acted when you and Colin began talking about the diary? When you did begin to discuss it, she first said everybody was daft and finally headed you off by suggesting that wretched whisky? And, of course, it did head you off. That's all."

Alan whistled.

"By gad, I believe you're right!"

"Thank you so much, dear. If you were to apply a little of that brain of yours," remarked Kathryn, wrinkling up her pretty nose, "to observing and drawing the inferences you're always telling everyone else to draw –"

Alan treated this with cold scorn. He had half a mind to make some reference to the Duchess of Cleveland, and the paucity of inference K.I. Campbell had been able to draw there, but he decided to give that unfortunate court lady a rest.

"Then the diary hasn't really anything to do with the case?"

"I wonder," said Dr Fell.

"Obviously," Kathryn pointed out, "Aunt Elspat knows *something*. And probably from the diary. Otherwise why all this business of writing to the *Daily Floodlight?*"

"Yes."

"And since she did write to them, it seems fairly clear that there wasn't anything in the diary to compromise her reputation. Then why on earth doesn't she speak out? What's the matter with her? If the diary gives some indication that Angus was murdered, why doesn't she say so?"

"Unless, of course," said Alan, "the diary says that he meant to commit suicide."

"Alan, Alan, Alan! To say nothing of all the other policies, Angus takes out a last policy, pays the premium, and then writes down that he's going to kill himself? It's just – against nature, that's all!"

Alan gloomily admitted this.

"Thirty-five thousand pounds in the balance," breathed Kathryn, "and she won't claim it. Why doesn't somebody tackle her about it? Why don't you tackle her, Dr Fell? Everybody else seems to be afraid of her."

"I shall be most happy," beamed Dr Fell.

Ponderously, like a man-o'-war easing into a dock, he turned round on the sofa. He adjusted his eyeglasses, and blinked at Elspat Campbell, who was standing in the doorway with an expression between wrath, pain, uncertainty, and the fear of damnation. They caught only the tail of this expression, which was gone in a flash, to be replaced by a tightening of the jaws and a determination of granite inflexibility.

Dr Fell was not impressed.

"Well, ma'am?" he inquired off-handedly. "You really did pinch that diary, didn't you?"

12

Twilight was deepening over Loch Fyne as they descended through the gray ghostly wood of fallen trees, and turned northwards along the main road to Shira.

Alan felt healthily and pleasantly tired after an afternoon in the open. Kathryn, in tweeds and flat-heeled shoes, had color in her cheeks and her blue eyes glowed. She had not once put on her spectacles for argument, even when she had been clucked at for being unfamiliar with the murder of the Red Fox, Colin Campbell of 1752, who had been shot by nobody knows whose hand, but for which James Stewart was tried at Inveraray courthouse.

"The trouble is," Alan was declaring, as they tramped down the hill, "Stevenson has so cast the glamour over us that we tend to forget what this 'hero,' this famous Alan Breck – one 'l,' please – was actually like. I've often wished somebody would take the side of the Campbells, for a change."

"Intellectual honesty again?"

"No. Just for fun. But the weirdest version of the incident was in the film version of *Kidnapped*. Alan Breck, and David Balfour, and a totally unnecessary female, are fleeing from the redcoats. Disguised up to the ears, they are driving in a cart

along a troop-infested road, singing 'Loch Lomond'; and Alan
Breck hisses, 'They'll never suspect us now.'

"I felt like arising and addressing the screen, saying: 'They
damn well will if you insist on singing a Jacobite song.' That's
about as sensible as though a group of British secret service
agents, disguised as Gestapo, were to swagger down Unter den
Linden singing, *There'll Always be an England*."

Kathryn seized on the essential part of this.

"So the female was totally unnecessary, eh?"

"What's that?"

"The female, says he in all his majesty, was totally unnecessary.
Of course!"

"I only mean that she wasn't in the original version, and she
spoiled what little story was left. Can't you forget this sex war for
five minutes?"

"It's you who are always dragging it in."

"Me?"

"Yes, you. I don't know what to make of you. You – you *can*
be rather nice, you know, when you try." She kicked the fallen
leaves out of her path, and suddenly began to giggle. "I was
thinking about last night."

"Don't remind me!"

"But that's when you were nicest, really. Don't you remember
what you said to me?"

He had thought the incident buried in merciful oblivion. It
was not.

"What did I say?"

"Never mind. We're terribly late for tea again, and Aunt
Elspat will carry on again, just as she did last night."

"Aunt Elspat," he said sternly, "Aunt Elspat, as you very well
know, won't be down to tea. She's confined to her room with a
violent and hysterical fit of the sulks."

Kathryn stopped and made a hopeless gesture.

"You know, I can't decide whether I like that old woman or

whether I'd like to murder her. Dr Fell tackles her about the diary, and all she does is go clear up in the air, and scream that it's her house, and she won't be bullied, and the dog carrier *was* under the bed –"

"Yes; but –"

"I think she just wants her own way. I think she won't tell anybody anything just because they want her to, and she's determined to be the boss. Just as she finished off in real sulks because Colin insisted on having that poor inoffensive Swan man in the house."

"Young lady, don't evade the question. What was it I said to you last night?"

The little vixen, he thought, was deliberately doing this. He wanted not to give her the satisfaction of showing curiosity. But he could not help it. They had come out into the main road only half a dozen yards from the Castle of Shira. Kathryn turned a demure but wicked-looking countenance in the twilight.

"If you can't remember," she told him innocently, "I can't repeat it to you. But I can tell you what my answer would have been, if I had made any answer."

"Well?"

"Oh, I should probably have said something like, 'In that case, why don't you?'"

Then she ran from him.

He caught up with her only in the hall, and there was no time to say anything more. The thunder of voices from the dining room would have warned them of what was in progress, even had they not caught sight of Colin through the partly open door.

The bright light shone over a snug table. Colin, Dr Fell, and Charles Swan had finished a very large meal. Their plates were pushed to one side, and in the center of the table stood a decanter bearing a rich brown liquid. On the faces of Dr Fell and Swan, before whom stood empty glasses, was the expression of men who have just passed through a great spiritual experience. Colin twinkled at them.

"Come in!" he cried to Kathryn and Alan. "Sit down. Eat before it gets cold. I've just been giving our friends their first taste of the Doom of the Campbells."

Swan's expression, preternaturally solemn, was now marred by a slight hiccup. But he remained solemn, and seemed to be meditating a profound experience.

His costume, too, was curious. He had been fitted out with one of Colin's shirts, which was too big in the shoulders and body, but much too short in the sleeves. Below this, since no pair of trousers in the house would fit him, he wore a kilt. It was the very dark green and blue of the Campbells, with thin transversing stripes of yellow and crossed-white.

"Cripes!" Swan muttered, contemplating the empty glass. "Cripes!"

"The observation," said Dr Fell, passing his hand across a pink forehead, "is not unwarranted."

"Like it?"

"Well –" said Swan.

"Have another? What about you, Alan? And you, Kitty-kat?"

"No." Alan was very firm about this. "I want some food. Maybe a little of that alcoholic tabasco sauce later, but a very little and not now."

Colin rubbed his hands.

"Oh, you will! They all do. What do you think of our friend Swan's getup? Neat, eh? I fished it out of a chest in the best bedroom. The original tartan of the Clan MacHolster."

Swan's face darkened.

"Are you kidding me?"

"As I believe in heaven," swore Colin, lifting his hand, "that's the MacHolster tartan as sure as I believe in heaven."

Swan was mollified. In fact, he seemed to be enjoying himself.

"It's a funny feeling," he said, eyeing the kilt. "Like walking around in public without your pants. Cripes, though! To think that I, Charley Swan of Toronto, should be wearing a real kilt in a real Scotch castle, and drinking old dew of the mountain like a clansman! I must write to my father about this. It's decent of you to let me stay all night."

"Nonsense! Your clothes won't be ready until morning, anyway. Have another?"

"Thanks. I don't mind if I do."

"You, Fell?"

"Harrumph," said Dr Fell. "That is an offer (or, in this case, challenge) I very seldom refuse. Thank'ee. But –"

"But what?"

"I was just wondering," said Dr Fell, crossing his knees with considerable effort, "whether the *nunc bibendum est* is to be followed by a reasonable *sat prata biberont*. In more elegant language, you're not thinking of another binge? Or have you given up the idea of sleeping in the tower tonight?"

Colin stiffened.

A vague qualm of uneasiness brushed the old room.

"And why should I give up the idea of sleeping in the tower?"

"It's just because I don't know why you shouldn't," returned Dr Fell frankly, "that I wish you wouldn't."

"Rubbish! I've spent half the afternoon repairing the lock and bolt of that door. I've carried my duds up there. You don't think *I'm* going to commit suicide?"

"Well," said Dr Fell, "suppose you did?"

The sense of uneasiness had grown greater. Even Swan seemed to feel it. Colin was about to break out into hollow incredulity, but Dr Fell stopped him.

"One moment. Merely suppose that. Or, to be more exact, suppose that tomorrow morning we find you dead at the foot of the tower under just such circumstances as Angus. Er – do you mind if I smoke while you're eating, Miss Campbell?"

"No, of course not," said Kathryn.

Dr Fell took out a large meerschaum pipe with a curved stem, which he filled from an obese pouch, and lighted. He sat back in his chair, argumentatively. With a somewhat cross-eyed expression behind his eyeglasses, he watched the smoke curl up into the bright bowl of the lamp.

"You believe," he went on, "you believe that your brother's death was murder: don't you?"

"I do! And I thundering well hope it was! If it was, and we can prove it, I inherit seventeen thousand five hundred pounds."

"Yes. But if Angus's death *was* murder, then the same force which killed Angus can kill you. Had you thought of that?"

"I'd like to see the force that could do it: God's wounds, I would!" snapped Colin.

But the calmness of Dr Fell's voice had its effect. Colin's tone was considerably more subdued.

"Now, if anything should by any chance happen to you," pursued Dr Fell, while Colin stirred, "what becomes of your share of the thirty-five thousand pounds? Does it revert to Elspat Campbell, for instance?"

"No, certainly not. It's kept in the family. It goes to Robert. Or to Robert's heirs if he's not alive."

"Robert?"

"Our third brother. He got into trouble and skipped the country years ago. We don't even know where he is, though Angus was always trying to find him. We do know he married and had children, the only one of us three who did marry. Robert would be – about sixty-four now. A year younger than I am."

Dr Fell continued to smoke meditatively, his eye on the lamp.

"You see," he wheezed, "assuming this to be murder, we have got to look for a motive. And a motive, on the financial side at least, is very difficult to find. Suppose Angus was murdered for his life-insurance money. By you. (Tut, now, don't jump down my throat!) Or by Elspat. Or by Robert or his heirs. Yet no murderer in his senses, under those circumstances, is going to plan a crime which will be taken for suicide, thereby depriving himself of the money which was the whole motive for the crime.

"So we come back to the personal. This man, Alec Forbes, now. I suppose he was capable of killing Angus?"

"Oh, Lord, yes!"

"H'm. Tell me. Has he got any grudge against you?"

Colin swelled with a kind of obscure satisfaction.

"Alec Forbes," Colin replied, "hates my guts almost as much as he hated Angus's. I ridiculed his schemes. And if there's one thing one of these moody chaps can't stand, it's ridicule. I never disliked the fellow myself, though."

"Yet you admit that the thing which killed Angus could kill you?"

Colin's neck hunched down into his shoulders. He stretched out his hand for the decanter of whisky. He poured out very large portions of it for Dr Fell, for Swan, for Alan, and for himself.

"If you're trying to persuade me not to sleep in the tower –"

"I am."

"Then be hanged to you. Because I'm going to." Colin scanned the faces round him with fiery eyes. "What's the matter with all of you?" he roared. "Are you all dead tonight? We had things better last night. Drink up! I'm not going to commit suicide; I promise you that. So drink up, and let's have no more of this tomfoolery now."

When they separated to go to bed at shortly past ten o'clock, not a man in that room was cold sober.

In gradations of sobriety they ranged from Swan, who had taken the stuff indiscreetly and could barely stand, to Dr Fell, whom nothing seemed to shake. Colin Campbell was definitely drunk, though his footstep was firm and only his reddish eyes betrayed him. But he was not drunk with the grinning, whooping abandon of the night before.

Nobody was. It had become one of those evenings when even the tobacco smoke turns stale and sour; and men, perversely, keep taking the final one which they don't need. When Kathryn slipped away before ten, no one attempted to stop her.

On Alan the liquor was having a wrong effect. Counteracting the weariness of his relaxed muscles, it stung him to tired but intense wakefulness. Thoughts scratched in his mind like pencils on slate; they would not go away or be still.

His bedroom was up on the first floor, overlooking the loch. His legs felt light as he ascended the stairs, saying good night to Dr Fell, who went to his own room (surprisingly) with magazines under his arm.

A lightness in the legs, a buzzing head, an intense discomfort, are no tonics for sleep. Alan groped into his room. Either out of economy or because of the sketchiness of the blackout, the chandelier contained no electric bulbs and only a candle could be used for illumination.

Alan lit the candle on the bureau. The meager little flame intensified the surrounding darkness, and made his face in the mirror look white. It seemed to him that he was tottering; that he was a fool to have touched that stuff again, since this time it brought neither exhilaration nor surcease.

Round and round whirled his thoughts, jumping from one point to another like clumsy mountain goats. People used to study by candlelight. It was a wonder they hadn't all gone blind. Maybe most of them had. He thought of Mr Pickwick in the Great White Horse at Ipswich. He thought of Scott ruining his eyesight by working under "a broad star of gas." He thought of . . .

It was no good. He *couldn't* sleep.

He undressed, stumbling, in the dark. He put on slippers and a dressing gown.

His watch ticked on. Ten-thirty. A quarter to eleven. The hour itself. Eleven-fifteen . . .

Alan sat down in a chair, put his head in his hands, and wished passionately for something to read. He had noticed very few books at Shira. Dr Fell, the doctor had informed him that day, had brought a *Boswell* along.

What a solace, what a soothing and comfort, *Boswell* would be now! To turn over those pages, to talk with Doctor Johnson until you drifted into a doze, must be the acme of all pleasure on this night. The more he thought of it, the more he wished he had it. Would Dr Fell lend it to him, for instance?

He got up, opened the door, and padded down a chilly hall to the doctor's room. He could have shouted for joy when he saw a thin line of light under the sill of the door. He knocked, and was told to come in in a voice which he hardly recognized as that of Dr Fell.

Alan, strung to a fey state of awareness, felt his scalp stir with terror as he saw the expression on Dr Fell's face.

Dr Fell sat by the chest of drawers, on top of which a candle was burning in its holder. He wore an old purple dressing gown as big as a tent. The meerschaum pipe hung from one corner of his mouth. Round him was scattered a heap of magazines, letters, and what looked like bills. Through a mist of tobacco smoke in the airless room, Alan saw the startled, far-away expression of Dr Fell's eyes, the open mouth which barely supported the pipe.

"Thank God you're here!" rumbled Dr Fell, suddenly coming to life. "I was just going to fetch you."

"Why?"

"I know what was in that box," said Dr Fell. "I know how the trick was worked. I know what set on Angus Campbell."

The candle flame wavered slightly among shadows. Dr Fell reached out for his crutch-handled stick, and groped wildly before he found it.

"We've got to get Colin out of that room," he added. "There may not be any danger; there probably isn't; but, by thunder, we can't afford to take any chances! I can show him now what did it, and he's got to listen to reason. See here."

Puffing and wheezing, he impelled himself to his feet.

"I underwent the martyrdom of climbing up those tower stairs once before today, but I can't do it again. Will you go up there and rout Colin out?"

"Of course."

"We needn't rouse anybody else. Just bang on the door until he lets you in; don't take no for an answer. Here. I've got a small torch. Keep it shielded when you go up the stairs, or you'll have the wardens after us. Hurry!"

"But what —"

"I haven't time to explain now. Hurry!"

Alan took the torch. Its thin, pale beam explored ahead of him. He went out in the hall, which smelled of old umbrellas, and down the stairs. A chilly draft touched his ankles. He crossed the lower hall, and went into the living-room.

Across the room, on the mantelpiece, the face of Angus Campbell looked back at him as the beam of his torch rested on the photograph. Angus's white, fleshy-jowled countenance seemed to stare back with the knowledge of a secret.

The door leading to the ground floor of the tower was locked on the inside. When Alan turned the squeaky key and opened the door, his fingers were shaking.

Now the earthen floor under him felt icy. A very faint mist had crept in from the loch. The arch leading to the tower stairs, a gloomy hole, repelled and somewhat unnerved him. Though he started to take the stairs at a run, both the dangerous footing and the exertion of the climb forced him to slow down.

First floor. Second floor, more of a pull. Third floor, and he was breathing hard. Fourth floor, and the distance up seemed endless. The little pencil of light intensified the coldness and close claustrophobia brought on by that enclosed space. It would not be pleasant to meet suddenly, on the stairs, a man in Highland costume with half his face shot away.

Or have the thing come out of one of the tower rooms, for instance, and touch him on the shoulder from behind.

You could not get away from anything that chose to pursue you here.

Alan reached the airless, windowless landing on which was the door to the topmost room. The oak door, its wood rather rotted by damp, was closed. Alan tried the knob, and found that it was locked and bolted on the inside.

He lifted his fist and pounded heavily on the door.

"Colin!" he shouted. "Colin!"

There was no reply.

The thunder of the knocking, the noise of his own voice, rebounded with infernal and intolerable racket in that confined space. He felt it must wake everybody in the house; everybody in Inveraray, for that matter. But he continued to knock and shout, still with no reply.

He set his shoulder to the door, and pushed. He got down on his knees and tried to peer under the sill of the door, but he could see nothing except an edge of moonlight.

As he got to his feet again, feeling light-headed after that exertion, the suspicion which had already struck him grew and grew with ugly effect. Colin *might* be only heavily asleep, of course, after all that whisky. On the other hand –

Alan turned round, and plunged down the treacherous stairs. The breath in his lungs felt like a rasping saw, and several times he had to pull up. He had even forgotten the Highlander. It seemed half an hour, and was actually two or three minutes, before he again reached the bottom of the stairs

The double doors leading out into the court were closed, but the padlock was not caught. Alan threw them open – creaking, quivering frames of wood which bent like bow shafts as they scraped the flagstones.

He ran out into the court, and circled round the tower to the side facing the loch. There he stopped short. He knew what he would find, and he found it.

The sickening plunge had been taken again.

Colin Campbell – or a bundle of red-and-white striped pyjamas which might once have been Colin – lay face downwards on the flagstones. Sixty feet above his head the leaves of the window stood open, and glinted by the light of the waning moon. A thin white mist, which seemed to hang above the water rather than rise from it, had made beads of dew settle on Colin's shaggy hair.

13

Dawn – warm gold and white kindling from smoky purple, yet of a soap-bubble luminousness which tinged the whole sky – dawn was clothing the valley when Alan again climbed the tower stairs. You could almost taste the early autumn air.

But Alan was in no mood to enjoy it.

He carried a chisel, an auger, and a saw. Behind him strode a nervous, wiry-looking Swan in a now-dry gray suit which had once been fashionable but which at present resembled sackcloth.

"But are you sure you want to go in there?" insisted Swan. "I'm not keen on it myself."

"Why not?" said Alan. "It's daylight. The Occupant of the box can't hurt us now."

"What occupant?"

Alan did not reply. He thought of saying that Dr Fell now knew the truth, though he had not divulged it yet; and that Dr Fell said there was no danger. But he decided such matters were best kept from the papers as yet.

"Hold the torch," he requested. "I can't see why they didn't put a window on this landing. Colin repaired this door yesterday afternoon, you remember. We're now going to arrange matters so that it can't be repaired again in a hurry."

While Swan held the light, he set to work. It was slow work, boring a line of holes touching each other in a square round the lock, and Alan's hands were clumsy on the auger.

When he had finished them, and splintered the result with a chisel, he got purchase for the saw and slowly sawed along the line of the holes.

"Colin Campbell," observed Swan, suddenly and tensely, "was a good guy. A real good guy."

"What do you mean, 'was'?"

"Now that he's dead –"

"But he's not dead."

There was an appreciable silence.

"*Not dead?*"

The saw rasped and bumped. All the violence of Alan's relief, all the sick reaction after what he had seen, went into his attack on the door. He hoped Swan would shut up. He had liked Colin Campbell immensely, too much to want to hear any sickly sentimentalities.

"Colin," he went on, without looking round to see Swan's expression, "has got two broken legs and a broken hipbone. And, for a man of his age, that's no joke. Also, there's something else Dr Grant is very much excited about. But he's not dead and he's unlikely to die."

"A fall like that –?"

"It happens sometimes. You've probably heard of people falling from heights greater than that and sometimes not even being hurt at all. And if they're tight, as Colin was, that helps too."

"Yet he deliberately jumped from the window?"

"Yes."

In a fine powdering of sawdust, the last tendon of wood fell free. Alan pushed the square panel inwards, and it fell on the floor. He reached through, finding the key still securely turned and the rusty bolt shot home immovably in its socket. He turned the key, pulled back the bolt; and, not without a qualm of apprehension, opened the door.

In the clear, fresh light of dawn, the room appeared tousled and faintly sinister. Colin's clothes, as he had untidily undressed, lay flung over the chairs and over the floor. His watch ticked on the chest of drawers. The bed had been slept in; its clothes were now flung back, and the pillows punched into a heap which still held the impression of a head.

The wide-open leaves of the window creaked gently as an air touched them.

"What are you going to do?" asked Swan, putting his head round the edge of the door and at last deciding to come in.

"What Dr Fell asked me to do."

Though he spoke easily enough, he had to get a grip on himself before he knelt down and felt under the bed. He drew out the leather dog carrier which had contained the Occupant.

"You're not going to fool around with this thing?" asked Swan.

"Dr Fell said to open it. He said there wouldn't be any fingerprints, so not to bother about them."

"You're taking a lot for granted on that old boy's word. But if you know what you're doing – open it."

This part was the hardest. Alan flicked back the catches with his thumbs, and lifted the lid.

As he had expected, the box was empty. Yet his imagination could have pictured, and was picturing, all sorts of unpleasant things he might have seen.

"What did the old boy tell you to do?" inquired Swan.

"Just open it, and make sure it was empty."

"But what *could* have been in it?" roared Swan. "I tell you, I'm going nuts trying to figure this thing out! I –" Swan paused. His eyes widened, and then narrowed. He extended a finger to point to the roll-top desk.

On the edge of the desk, half-hidden by papers but in a place where it certainly had not been the day before, lay a small leather book of pocket size, on whose cover was stamped, in gilt letters, *Diary, 1940.*

"That wouldn't be what you've been looking for, would it?"

Both of them made a dart for the diary, but Alan got there first.

The name Angus Campbell was written on the fly-leaf in a small but stiff and schoolboyish kind of hand which made Alan suspect arthritis in the fingers. Angus had carefully filled out the chart for all the miscellaneous information, such as the size of his collar and the size of his shoes (why the makers of these diaries think we are likely to forget the size of our collars remains a mystery); and after "motorcar license number" he had written "none."

But Alan did not bother with this. The diary was full of entries all crammed together and crammed downhill. The last entry was made on the night of Angus's death, Saturday the twenty-fourth of August. Alan Campbell became conscious of tightened throat muscles, and a heavy thumping in his chest, as his eye encountered the item.

Saturday. Check cleared by bank. OK. Elspat poorly again. Memo: syrup of figs. Wrote to Colin. A. Forbes here tonight. Claims I cheated him. Ha ha ha. Said not to come back. He said he wouldn't, wasn't necessary. Funny musty smell in room tonight. Memo: write to War Office about tractor. Use for army. Do this tomorrow.

Then there was the blank which indicated the end of the writer's span of life.

Alan flicked back over the pages. He did not read any more, though he noticed that at one point a whole leaf had been torn out. He was thinking of the short, heavy, bulbous-nosed old man with the white hair, writing these words while something waited for him.

"H'm," said Swan. "That isn't much help, is it?"

"I don't know."

"Well," said Swan, "if you've seen what you came to see, or rather what you didn't see, let's get downstairs again, shall we? There may be nothing wrong with this place, but it gives me the willies."

Slipping the diary into his pocket, Alan gathered up the tools and followed. In the sitting-room downstairs they found Dr Fell, fully dressed in an old black alpaca suit and string tie. Alan noticed with surprise that his box-pleated cape and shovel-hat lay across the sofa, whereas last night they had hung in the hall.

But Dr Fell appeared to be violently interested in a very bad landscape hung above the piano. He turned round a guileless face at their entrance, and addressed Swan.

"I say. Would you mind nipping up to – harrumph – what we'll call the sick-room, and finding out how the patient is? Don't let Dr Grant bully you. I want to find out whether Colin's conscious yet, and whether he's said anything."

"So do I," agreed Swan with some vehemence, and was off with such celerity as to make the pictures rattle.

Dr Fell hastily picked up his box-pleated cape, swung it round his shoulders with evident effort, and fastened the little chain at the neck.

"Get your hat, my lad," he said. "We're off on a little expedition. The presence of the press is no doubt stimulating, but there are times when it is definitely an encumbrance. We may be able to speak out without our friend Swan seeing us."

"Where are we going?"

"Glencoe."

Alan stared at him.

"Glencoe! At seven o'clock in the morning?"

"I regret," sighed Dr Fell, sniffing the odor of frying bacon and eggs which had begun to seep through the house, "that we shall not be able to wait for breakfast. But better miss breakfast than spoil the whole broth."

"Yes, but how in blazes are we going to get to Glencoe at this hour?"

"I've phoned through to Inveraray for a car. They haven't your slothful habits in this part of the country, my lad. Do you remember Duncan telling us yesterday that Alec Forbes had been found, or they thought he had been found, at a cottage near Glencoe?"

"Yes?"

Dr Fell made a face and flourished his crutch-handled stick.

"It may not be true. And we may not even be able to find the cottage: though I got a description of its location from Duncan, and habitations out there are few and far between. But, by thunder, we've got to take the chance! If I'm to be any good to Colin Campbell at all, I've GOT to reach Alec Forbes before anybody else – even the police – can get to him. Get your hat."

Kathryn Campbell, pulling on her tweed jacket, moved swiftly into the room.

"Oh, no, you don't!" she said.

"Don't what?"

"You don't go without me," Kathryn informed them. "I heard you ringing up for that car. Aunt Elspat is bossy enough anywhere, but Aunt Elspat in a sick-room is simply bossy past all endurance. Eee!" She clenched her hands. "There's nothing more I can do anyhow. *Please* let me come!"

Dr Fell waved a gallant assent. Tiptoeing like conspirators, they moved out to the back of the house. A brightly polished four-seater car was waiting beyond the hedge which screened Shira from the main road.

Alan did not want a loquacious chauffeur that morning, and he did not get one. The driver was a gnarled little man, dressed like a garage mechanic, who grudgingly held open the door for them. They were past Dalmally before they discovered that he was, in fact, an English cockney.

But Alan was too full of his latest discovery to mind the presence of a witness. He produced Angus's diary, and handed it to Dr Fell.

Even on an empty stomach, Dr Fell had filled and lighted his meerschaum. It was an open car, and as it climbed the mighty hill under a somewhat damp-looking sky, the breeze gave Dr Fell considerable trouble in its attentions to his hat and the tobacco smoke. But he read carefully through the diary, giving at least a glance at every page of it.

"H'mf, yes," he said, and scowled. "It fits. Everything fits! Your deductions, Miss Campbell, were to the point. It *was* Elspat who stole this."

"But –"

"Look here." He pointed to the place where a page had been torn out. "The entry before that, at the foot of the preceding page, reads, 'Elspat says Janet G' – whoever she may be – 'godless and lecherous. In Elspat's younger days –' There it breaks off.

"It probably went on to recount gleefully an anecdote of Elspat's younger and less moral days. So the evidence was removed from the record. Elspat found nothing more in the diary to reflect on her. After giving it a careful reading, probably several readings to make sure, she returned the diary to a place where it could easily be found."

Alan was not impressed.

"Still, what about these sensational revelations? Why get in touch with the press, as Elspat did? The last entry in the diary may be suggestive, but it certainly doesn't tell us very much."

"No?"

"Well, does it?"

Dr Fell eyed him curiously.

"I should say, on the contrary, that it tells us a good deal. But you hardly expected the sensational revelation (if any) to be in the last entry, did you? After all, Angus had gone happily and thoughtlessly to bed. Whatever attacked him, it attacked him after he had finished writing and put out his light. Why, therefore, should we expect anything of great interest in the last entry?"

Alan was brought up with something of a bump.

"That," he admitted, "is true enough. All the same –"

"No, my boy. The real meat of the thing is *here*" Dr Fell made the pages riffle like a pack of cards. "In the body of the diary. In the account of his activities for the past year."

He frowned at the book, and slipped it into his pocket. His expression of gargantuan distress had grown along with his fever of certainty.

"Hang it all!" he said, and smote his hand on his knee. "The thing is inescapable! Elspat steals the diary. She reads it. Being no fool, she guesses –"

"Guesses what?"

"How Angus Campbell really died. She hates and distrusts the police to the very depths of her soul. So she writes to her favorite newspaper and plans to explode a bomb. And suddenly, when it is too late, she realizes with horror –"

Again Dr Fell paused. The expression on his face smoothed itself out. He sat back with a gusty sigh against the upholstery of the tonneau, and shook his head.

"You know, that tears it," he added blankly. "That really does tear it."

"I personally," Kathryn said through her teeth, "will be in a condition to tear something if this mystification goes on."

Dr Fell appeared still more distressed.

"Allow me," he suggested, "to counter your very natural curiosity with just one more question." He looked at Alan. "A moment ago you said that you thought the last entry in Angus's diary was 'suggestive.' What did you mean by that?"

"I meant that it certainly wasn't a passage which could have been written by anyone who meant to kill himself."

Dr Fell nodded.

"Yes," he agreed. "Then what would you say if I were to tell you that Angus Campbell really committed suicide after all?"

14

"I should reply," said Kathryn, "that I felt absolutely cheated! Oh, I know I shouldn't say that; but it's true. You've got us looking so hard for a murderer that we can't concentrate on anything else."

Dr Fell nodded as though he saw the aesthetic validity of the point.

"And yet," he went on, "for the sake of argument, I ask you to consider this explanation. I ask you to observe how it is borne out by every one of our facts."

He was silent for a moment, puffing at the meerschaum.

"Let us first consider Angus Campbell. Here is a shrewd, embittered, worn-out old man with a tinkering brain and an intense love of family. He is now broke, stony broke. His great dreams will never come true. He knows it. His brother Colin, of whom he is very fond, is overwhelmed with debts. His ex-mistress Elspat, of whom he is fonder still, is penniless and will remain penniless.

"Angus might well consider himself, in the hard-headed Northern fashion, a useless encumbrance. Good to nobody – except dead. But he is a hale old body to whom the insurance company's doctor gives fifteen more years of life. And in the meantime how (in God's name, how) are they to live?

"Of course, if he were to die now . . ."

Dr Fell made a slight gesture.

"But, if he dies now, it must be established as certain, absolutely *certain*, that his death is not a suicide. And that will take a bit of doing. The sum involved is huge: thirty-five thousand pounds, distributed among intelligent insurance companies with nasty suspicious minds.

"Mere accident won't do. He can't go out and stumble off a cliff, hoping it will be read as accident. They might think that; but it is too chancy, and nothing must be left to chance. His death must be murder, cold-blooded murder, proved beyond any shadow of a doubt."

Again Dr Fell paused. Alan improved the occasion to utter a derisive laugh which was not very convincing.

"In that case, sir," Alan said, "I turn your own guns on you."

"So? How?"

"You asked last night why any person intending to commit a murder for the insurance money should commit a murder which looked exactly like suicide. Well, for the same reason, why should Angus (of all people) plan a suicide which looked exactly like suicide?"

"He didn't," answered Dr Fell.

"Pardon?"

Dr Fell leaned forward to tap Alan, who occupied the front seat, very decisively on the shoulder. The doctor's manner was compounded of eagerness and absentmindedness.

"That's the whole point. He didn't. You see, you haven't yet realized what was in that dog carrier. You haven't yet realized what Angus deliberately put there.

"And I say to you" – Dr Fell lifted his hand solemnly – "I say to you that but for one little unforeseeable accident, a misfortune so unlikely that the mathematical chances were a million to one against it, there would never have been the least doubt that Angus was murdered! I say to you that Alec Forbes would be in jail at this moment, and that the insurance companies would have been compelled to pay up."

They were approaching Loch Awe, a gem of beauty in a deep, mountainous valley. But none of them looked at it.

"Are you saying," breathed Kathryn, "that Angus was going to kill himself, and deliberately frame Alec Forbes for the job?"

"I am. Do you consider it unlikely?"

After a silence Dr Fell went on.

"In the light of this theory, consider our evidence.

"Here is Forbes, a man with a genuine, bitter grudge. Ideal for the purposes of a scapegoat.

"Forbes calls – for which we may read, 'is summoned' – to see Angus that night. He goes upstairs to the tower room. There is a row, which Angus can arrange to make audible all over the place. Now, was Forbes at this time carrying a 'suitcase'?

"The women, we observe, don't know. They didn't see him until he was ejected. Who is the only witness to the suitcase? Angus himself. He carefully calls their attention to the fact that Forbes was supposed to have one, *and* says pointedly that Forbes must have left it behind.

"You follow that? The picture Angus intended to present was that Forbes had distracted his attention and shoved the suitcase under the bed, where Angus never noticed it, but where the thing inside it could later do its deadly work."

Alan reflected.

"It's a curious thing," Alan said, "that the day before yesterday I myself suggested just that explanation, with Forbes as the murderer. But nobody would listen to it."

"Yet I repeat," asserted Dr Fell, "that except for a totally unpredictable accident, Forbes would have been nailed as the murderer straightaway."

Kathryn put her hands to her temples.

"You mean," she cried, "that Elspat looked under the bed before the door was locked, and saw there was no box there?"

But to their surprise Dr Fell shook his head.

"No, no, no, no! That was another point, of course. But it wasn't serious. Angus probably never even thought her glance under the bed noticed anything one way or the other. No, no, no! I refer to the contents of the box."

Alan closed his eyes.

"I suppose," he said in a restrained voice, "it would be asking too much if we were to ask you just to *tell* us what was in the box?"

Dr Fell grew still more solemn, even dogged.

"In a very short time we are (I hope) going to see Alec Forbes. I am going to put the question to him. In the meantime, I ask you to think about it; think about the facts we know; think about the trade magazines in Angus's room; think about his activities of the past year; and see if you can't reach the solution for yourselves.

"For the moment let us return to the great scheme. Alec Forbes, of course, had carried no suitcase or anything else. The box (already prepared by Angus himself) was downstairs in one of the lower rooms. Angus got rid of the women at ten o'clock, slipped downstairs, procured the box, and put it under the bed, after which he relocked and rebolted his door. This, I submit, is the only possible explanation of how that box got into a hermetically sealed room.

"Finally, Angus wrote up his diary. He put in those significant words that he had told Forbes not to come back, and Forbes said it wouldn't be necessary. Other significant words too: so many more nails in Forbes's coffin. Then Angus undressed, turned out the light, climbed into bed, and with real grim fortitude prepared for what had to come.

"Now follow what happens next day. Angus has left his diary in plain sight, for the police to find. Elspat finds it herself, and appropriates it.

"She thinks Alec Forbes killed Angus. On reading through the bulk of the diary, she realizes – as Angus meant everybody to realize – exactly what killed Angus. She has got Alec Forbes, the murderer. She will hang the sinful higher than Haman. She sits down and writes to the *Daily Floodlight*.

"Only after the letter is posted does she suddenly see the flaw. If Forbes did that, he must have pushed the box under the bed before he was kicked out. But Forbes can't have done that! For she herself looked under the bed, and saw no box; and, most horrifying of all, she has already told the police so."

Dr Fell made a gesture.

"This woman has lived with Angus Campbell for forty years. She knows him inside out. She sees through him with that almost morbid clarity our womenfolk exhibit in dealing with our vagaries and our stupidities. It doesn't take her long to understand where the hanky-panky lies. It wasn't Alec Forbes; it was Angus himself who did this. And so –

"Do I have to explain further? Think over her behavior. Think of her sudden change of mind about the box. Think of her searching for excuses to fly into a tantrum and throw out of the house the newspaperman she has summoned herself. Think, above all, of her position. If she speaks out with the truth, she loses every penny. If she denounces Alec Forbes, on the other hand, she condemns her soul to hellfire and eternal burning. Think of that, my children; and don't be too hard on Elspat Campbell when her temper seems to wear thin."

The figure of one whom Kathryn had called a silly old woman was undergoing, in their minds, a curious transformation.

Thinking back to eyes and words and gestures, thinking of the core under that black taffeta, Alan experienced a revulsion of feeling as well as a revulsion of ideas.

"And so –?" he prompted.

"Well! She won't make the decision," replied Dr Fell. "She returns the diary to the tower room, and lets us decide what we like."

The car had climbed to higher, bleaker regions. Uplands of

waste, spiked with ugly posts against possible invasion by air, showed brown against the granite ribs of the mountains. The day was clouding over, and a damp breeze blew in their faces.

"May I submit," Dr Fell added after a pause, "that this is the only explanation which fits all the facts?"

"Then if we're not looking for a murderer –"

"Oh, my dear sir!" expostulated Dr Fell. "We *are* looking for a murderer!"

They whirled round on him.

"Ask yourselves other questions," said Dr Fell. "Who impersonated the ghostly Highlander, and why? Who sought the death of Colin Campbell, and why? For remember: except for lucky chance, Colin would be dead at this minute."

He brooded, chewing the stem of a pipe that had gone out, and making a gesture as though he were pursuing something which just eluded him.

"Pictures," he added, "sometimes give extraordinary ideas."

Then he seemed to realize for the first time that he was talking in front of an outsider. He caught, in the driving mirror, the eye of the gnarled little chauffeur who for miles had not spoken or moved. Dr Fell rumbled and snorted, brushing fallen ash off his cape. He woke up out of a mazy dream, and blinked round.

"H'mf. Hah. Yes. So. I say, when do we get to Glencoe?"

The driver spoke out of the side of his mouth.

"This *is* Glencoe," he answered.

All of them woke up.

And here, Alan thought, were the wild mountains as he had always imagined them. The only adjective which occurred in connection with the place was God-forsaken: not as an idle word, but as a literal fact.

The glen of Coe was immensely long and immensely wide, whereas Alan had always pictured it as a cramped, narrow place. Through it the black road ran arrow-straight. On either side rose the lines of mountain-ridges, granite-gray and dull purple, looking as smooth as stone. No edge of kindliness touched them: it was as though nature had dried up, and even sullenness had long petrified to hostility.

Burns twisting down the mountain-side were so far off that you could not even be sure if the water moved, and only were sure when you saw it gleam. Utter silence emphasized the bleakness and desolation of the glen. Sometimes you saw a tiny whitewashed cottage, which appeared empty.

Dr Fell pointed to one of them.

"We are looking," he said, "for a cottage on the left-hand side of the road, down a slope among some fir trees, just past the Falls of Coe. You don't happen to know it?"

The driver was silent for a time, and then said he thought he knew it.

"Not far off now," he added. "Be at the Falls in a minute or two."

The road rose, and, after its interminable straightness, curved round the slaty shoulder of a hill. The hollow, tumbling roar of a waterfall shook the damp air as they turned into a narrow road, shut in on the right by a cliff.

Driving them some distance down this road, the chauffeur stopped the car, sat back, and pointed without a word.

They climbed out on the breezy road, under a darkening sky. The tumult of the waterfall still splashed in their ears. Dr Fell was assisted down a slope on which they all slithered. He was assisted, with more effort, across a stream; and in the bed of the stream, the stones were polished black, as though they had met the very heart of the soil.

The cottage, of dirty whitewashed stone with a thatched roof, stood beyond. It was tiny, appearing to consist of only one room. The door stood closed. No smoke went up from the chimney. Far beyond it the mountains rose up light purple and curiously pink.

Nothing moved – except a mongrel dog.

The dog saw them, and began to run round in circles. It darted to the cottage, and scratched with its paws on the closed door. The scratching sound rose thinly, above the distant mutter of the falls. It set a seal on the heart, of loneliness and depression in the evil loneliness of Glencoe.

The dog sat back on its haunches, and began to howl.

"All right, old boy!" said Dr Fell.

That reassuring voice seemed to have some effect on the animal. It scratched frantically at the door again, after which it ran to Dr Fell and capered round him, leaping up to scrape at his cloak. What frightened Alan was the fright in the eyes of the dog.

Dr Fell knocked at the door, without response. He tried the latch, but something held the door on the inside. There was no window in the front of the cottage.

"Mr Forbes!" he called thunderously. "Mr Forbes!"

Their footsteps scraped amidst little flinty stones. The shape of the cottage was roughly square. Muttering to himself, Dr Fell lumbered round to the side of the house, and Alan followed him.

Here they found a smallish window. A rusty metal grating, like a mesh of heavy wire, had been nailed up over the window on the inside. Beyond this its grimy windowpane, set on hinges to swing open and shut like a door, stood partly open.

Cupping their hands round their eyes, they pressed against the grating and tried to peer inside. A frowsty smell, compounded of stale air, stale whisky, paraffin oil, and sardines out of a tin, crept out of the room. Gradually, as their eyes grew accustomed to the gloom, outlines emerged.

The table, with its greasy mess of dishes, had been pushed to one side. In the center of the ceiling was set a stout iron hook, presumably for a lamp. Alan saw what was hanging from that hook now, and swaying gently each time the dog pawed at the door.

He dropped his hands. He turned away from the window, putting one hand against the wall to steady himself. He walked round the side of the cottage to the front, where Kathryn was standing.

"What is it?" He heard her voice distantly, though it was almost a scream. "What's wrong?"

"You'd better come away from here," he said.

"What is it?"

Dr Fell, much less ruddy of face, followed Alan round to the front door.

The doctor breathed heavily and wheezily for a moment before he spoke.

"That's rather a flimsy door," he said, pointing with his stick. "You could kick it in. And I think you better had."

On the inside was a small, new, tight bolt. Alan tore the staple loose from the wood with three vicious kicks into which he put his whole muscle and the whole state of his mind.

Though he was not anxious to go inside, the face of the dead man was now turned away from them, and it was not so bad as the first look through the window. The smell of food and whisky and paraffin grew overpowering.

The dead man wore a long, grimy dressing gown. The rope, which had formed the plaited cord of his dressing gown, had been shaped at one end into a running noose, and the other tied tightly round the hook in the ceiling. His heels swung some two feet off the floor as he hung there. An empty keg, evidently of whisky, had rolled away from under him.

Whining frenziedly, the mongrel dog shot past them, whirled round the dead man, and set him swinging again in frantic attempts to spring up.

Dr Fell inspected the broken bolt. He glanced across at the grated window. His voice sounded heavy in the evil-smelling room.

"Oh, yes," he said. "Another suicide."

15

"I suppose," Alan muttered, "it *is* Alec Forbes?"

Dr Fell pointed with his stick to the camp-bed pushed against one wall. On it an open suitcase full of soiled linen bore the painted initials "A.G.F." Then he walked round to the front of the hanging figure where he could examine the face. Alan did not follow him.

"And the description fits, too. A week's growth of beard on his face. And, in all probability, ten years' growth of depression in his heart."

Dr Fell went to the door, barring it against Kathryn, who stood white-faced under the overcast sky a few feet away.

"There must be a telephone somewhere. If I remember my map, there's a village with a hotel a mile or two beyond here. Get through to Inspector Donaldson at Dunoon police station, and tell him Mr Forbes has hanged himself. Can you do that?"

Kathryn gave a quick, unsteady nod.

"He did kill himself, did he?" she asked in a voice barely above a whisper. "It isn't – anything else?"

Dr Fell did not reply to this. Kathryn, after another quick nod, turned and made her way back.

The hut was some dozen feet square, thick-walled, with a

primitive fireplace and a stone floor. It was no crofter's cottage, but had evidently been used by Forbes as a sort of retreat. Its furniture consisted of the camp bed, the table, two kitchen chairs, a washstand with bowl and pitcher, and a stand of mildewed books.

The mongrel had now ceased its frantic whimpering, for which Alan felt grateful. The dog lay down close to the silent figure, where he could raise adoring eyes to that altered face; and, from time to time, he shivered.

"I ask what Kathryn asked," said Alan. "Is this suicide, or not?"

Dr Fell walked forward and touched Forbes' arm. The dog stiffened. A menacing growl began in its throat and quivered through its whole body.

"Easy, boy!" said Dr Fell. "Easy!"

He stood back. He took out his watch and studied it. Grunting and muttering, he lumbered over to the table, on whose edge stood a hurricane lantern with a hook and chain by which it could be slung from the roof. With the tips of his fingers Dr Fell picked up the lantern and shook it. A tin of oil stood beside it.

"Empty," he said. "Burned out, but obviously used." He pointed to the body. "Rigor is not complete. This undoubtedly happened during the early hours of the morning: two or three o'clock, perhaps. The hour of suicides. And look there."

He was now pointing to the plaited dressing-gown cord around the dead man's neck.

"It's a curious thing," he went on, scowling. "The genuine suicide invariably takes the most elaborate pains to guard himself against the least discomfort. If he hangs himself, for instance, he will never use a wire or chain: something that is likely to cut or chafe his neck. If he uses a rope, he will often pad it against chafing. Look there! Alec Forbes has used a soft rope, and padded that with handkerchiefs. The authentic touch of suicide, or –"

"Or what?"

"Real genius in murder," said Dr Fell.

He bent down to inspect the empty whisky-keg. He went across to the one window. Thrusting one finger through the mesh of the grating, he shook it and found it solidly nailed up on the inside. Back he went, with fussed and fussy gestures, to the bolt of the door, which he examined carefully without touching it.

Then he peered round the room, stamping his foot on the floor. His voice had taken on a hollow sound like wind along an Underground tunnel.

"Hang it all!" he said. "This *is* suicide. It's got to be suicide. The keg is just the right height for him to have stepped off, and just the right distance away. Nobody could have got in or out through that nailed window or that solidly bolted door."

He regarded Alan with some anxiety.

"You see, for my sins I know something about hocusing doors or windows. I have been – ahem – haunted and pursued by such matters."

"So I've heard."

"But I can't," pursued Dr Fell, pushing back his shovel hat, "I can't tell you any way of hocusing a bolt when there's no keyhole and when the door is so close-fitting that its sill scrapes the floor. Like that one."

He pointed.

"And I can't tell you any way of hocusing a window when it is covered with a steel mesh-work nailed up on the inside. Again, like that one there. If Alec Forbes – hullo!"

The bookstand was placed cater-cornered in the angle beside the fireplace. Dr Fell discovered it as he went to inspect the fireplace, finding to his disgust that the flue was too narrow and soot-choked to admit any person. Dusting his fingers, he turned to the bookstand.

On the top row of books stood a portable typewriter, its cover missing and a sheet of paper projecting from the carriage. On it a few words were typed in pale blue ink.

To any jackal who finds this:

I killed Angus and Colin Campbell with the same thing they used to swindle me. What are you going to do about it now?

"Even, you see," Dr Fell said fiercely, "the suicide note. The final touch. The brush-stroke of the master. I repeat, sir: this must be suicide. And yet – well, if it is, I mean to retire to Bedlam."

The smell of the room, the black-faced occupant, the yearning dog, all these things were commencing to turn Alan Campbell's stomach. He felt he could not stand the air of the place much longer. Yet he fought back.

"I don't see why you say that," he declared. "After all, Doctor, can't you admit you may be wrong?"

"Wrong?"

"About Angus's death being suicide." Certainty, dead certainty, took root in Alan Campbell's brain. "Forbes *did* kill Angus and tried to kill Colin. Everything goes to show it. Nobody could have got in or out of this room, as you yourself admit; and there's Forbes's confession to clinch matters.

"He brooded out here until his brain cracked, as I know mine would in these parts unless I took to religion. He disposed of both brothers, or thought he had. When his work was finished, he killed himself. Here's the evidence. What more do you want?"

"The truth," insisted Dr Fell stubbornly. "I am old-fashioned. I want the truth."

Alan hesitated.

"I'm old-fashioned too. And I seem to remember," Alan told him, "that you came north with the express purpose of helping Colin. Is it going to help Colin, or Aunt Elspat either, if the detective they brought in to show Angus was murdered goes about showing that it was suicide – even after we've got Alec Forbes's confession?"

Dr Fell blinked at him.

"My dear sir," he said in pained astonishment, and adjusted his eyeglasses and blinked at Alan through them, "you surely don't imagine that I mean to confide any of my beliefs to the police?"

"Isn't that the idea?"

Dr Fell peered about to make sure they were not overheard.

"My record," he confided, "is an extremely black one. Harrumph. I have on several occasions flummoxed the evidence so that a murderer should go free. Not many years ago I outdid myself by setting a house on fire. My present purpose (between ourselves) is to swindle the insurance companies so that Colin Campbell can bask in good cigars and fire-water for the rest of his life . . ."

"*What?*"

Dr Fell regarded him anxiously.

"That shocks you? Tut, tut! All this (I say) I mean to do. But, dammit, man!" He spread out his hands. "For my own private information, I like to know the truth."

He turned back to the bookstand. Still without touching it, he examined the typewriter. On top of the row of books below it stood an angler's creel and some salmon flies. On top of the third row of books lay a bicycle spanner, a bicycle lamp, and a screwdriver.

Dr Fell next ran a professional eye over the books. There were works on physics and chemistry, on Diesel engines, on practical building, and on astronomy. There were catalogs and trade journals. There was a dictionary, a six-volume encyclopedia, and (surprisingly) two or three boys' books by G.A. Henty. Dr Fell eyed these last with some interest.

"Wow!" he said. "Does anybody read Henty nowadays, I wonder? If they knew what they were missing, they would run back to him. I am proud to say that I still read him with delight. Who would suspect Alec Forbes of having a romantic soul?" He scratched his nose. "Still —"

"Look here," Alan persisted. "What makes you so sure this isn't suicide?"

"My theory. My mule-headedness, if you prefer it."

"And your theory still holds that Angus committed suicide?"

"Yes."

"But that Forbes here was murdered?"

"Exactly."

Dr Fell wandered back to the center of the room. He eyed the untidy camp-bed with the suitcase on it. He eyed a pair of gum-boots under the bed.

"My lad, I don't trust that suicide note. I don't trust it one little bit. And there are solid reasons why I don't trust it. Come out here. Let's get some clean air."

Alan was glad enough to go. The dog raised its head from its paws, and gave them a wild, dazed sort of look; then it lowered its head again, growling, and settled down with ineffable patience under the dead.

Distantly, they could hear the rushing of the waterfall. Alan breathed the cool, damp air, and felt a shudder go over him. Dr Fell, a huge bandit shape in his cloak, leaned his hands on his stick.

"Whoever wrote that note," he went on, "whether Alec Forbes or another, knew the trick that had been employed in Angus Campbell's death. That's the first fact to freeze to. Well! Have you guessed yet what the trick was?"

"No, I have not."

"Not even after seeing the alleged suicide note? Oh, man! Think!"

"You can ask me to think all you like. I may be dense; but if you can credit it, I still don't know what makes people jump up out of bed in the middle of the night and fall out of windows to their death."

"Let us begin," pursued Dr Fell, "with the fact that Angus's diary records his activities for the past year, as diaries sometimes do. Well, what in Satan's name *have* been Angus's principal activities for the past year?"

"Mixing himself up in various wildcat schemes to try to make money."

"True. But only one scheme in which Alec Forbes was concerned, I think?"

"Yes."

"Good. What was that scheme?"

"An idea to manufacture some kind of ice cream with tartan patterns on it. At least, so Colin said."

"And in making their ice cream," said Dr Fell, "what kind of freezing agent did they employ in large quantities? Colin told us that too."

"He said they used artificial ice, which he described as 'that chemical stuff that's so expen –'"

Alan paused abruptly.

Half-forgotten memories flowed back into his mind. With a shock he recalled a laboratory of his school days, and words being spoken from a platform. The faint echo of them came back now.

"And do you know," inquired Dr Fell, "what this artificial ice, or 'dry' ice, really is?"

"It's whitish stuff to look at; something like real ice, only opaque. It –"

"To be exact," said Dr Fell, "it is nothing more or less than liquefied gas. And do you know the name of the gas which is turned into a solid 'snow' block, and can be cut and handled and moved about? What is the name of that gas?"

"Carbon dioxide," said Alan.

Though the spell remained on his wits, it was suddenly as though a blind had flown up with a snap, and he saw.

"Now suppose," argued Dr Fell, "you removed a block of that stuff from its own airtight cylinders. A big block, say one big enough to fit into a large suitcase – or, better still, some box with an open end, so that the air can reach it better. What would happen?"

"It would slowly melt."

"And in melting, of course, it would release into the room . . . what would it release?"

Alan found himself almost shouting.

"Carbonic acid gas. One of the deadliest and quickest-acting gases there is."

"Suppose you placed your artificial ice, in its container, under the bed in a room where the window is always kept closed at night. What would happen?

"With your permission, I will now drop the Socratic method and tell you. You have planted one of the surest murder traps ever devised. One of two things will happen. Either the victim, asleep or drowsy, will breathe in that concentrated gas as it is released into the room; and he will die in his bed.

"Or else the victim will notice the faint, acrid odor as it gets into his lungs. He will not breathe it long, mind you. Once the stuff takes hold, it will make the strongest man totter and fall like a fly. He will want air – air at any cost. As he is overcome, he will get out of bed and try to make for the window.

"He may not make it at all. If he does make it, he will be so weak on the legs that he can't hold up. And if this window is a low window, catching him just above the knees; if it consists of two leaves, opening outwards, so that he falls against it –"

Dr Fell pushed his hands outwards, a rapid gesture.

Alan could almost see the limp, unwieldy body in the nightshirt plunge outwards and downwards.

"Of course, the artificial ice will melt away and leave no trace in the box. With the window now open, the gas will presently clear away.

"You now perceive, I hope, why Angus's suicide scheme was so foolproof. Who but Alec Forbes would have used artificial ice to kill his partner in the venture?

"Angus, as I read it, never once intended to jump or fall from the window. No, no, no! He intended to be found dead in bed, of poisoning by carbonic acid gas. There would be a post-mortem. The 'hand' of this gas would be found in his blood as plain as print. The diary would be read and interpreted. All the circumstances against Alec Forbes would be recalled, as I outlined them to you awhile ago. And the insurance money would be collected as certainly as the sun will rise tomorrow."

Alan, staring at the stream, nodded.

"But at the last moment, I suppose –?"

"At the last moment," agreed Dr Fell, "like many suicides, Angus couldn't face it. He had to have *air*. He felt himself going under. And in a panic he leaped for the window.

"Therein, my boy, lies the million-to-one chance I spoke of. It was a million to one that either (*a*) the gas would kill him, or (*b*) the fall would kill him instantly as he plunged out face forwards. But neither of these things happened. He was mortally injured; yet he did not immediately die. Remember?"

Again Alan nodded.

"Yes. We've come across that point several times."

"Before he died, his lungs and blood were freed of the gas. Hence no trace remained for the post-mortem. Had he died instantly or even quickly, those traces would have been there. But they were not. So we had only the meaningless spectacle of an old gentleman who leaps from his bed in order to throw himself out of the window."

Dr Fell's big voice grew fiery. He struck the ferrule of his stick on the ground.

"I say to you –" he began.

"Stop a bit!" said Alan, with sudden recollection.

"Yes?"

"Last night, when I went up to the tower room to rout out Colin, I bent down and tried to look under the still of the door. When I straightened up, I remember feeling lightheaded. In fact,

155

I staggered when I went down the stairs. Did *I* get a whiff of the stuff?"

"Of course. The room was full of it. Only a very faint whiff, fortunately for yourself.

"Which brings us to the final point. Angus carefully wrote in his diary that there was a 'faint musty smell in the room.' Now, that's rubbish on the face of it. If he had already begun to notice the presence of the gas, he could never have completed his diary and gone to bed. No: that was only another artistic touch designed to hang Alec Forbes."

"And misinterpreted by me," growled Alan. "I was thinking about some kind of animal."

"But you see where all this leads us?"

"No, I don't. Into the soup, of course; but aside from that –"

"The only possible explanation of the foregoing facts," insisted Dr Fell, "is that Angus killed himself. If Angus killed himself, then Alec Forbes didn't kill him. And if Alec Forbes didn't kill him, Alec had no reason to say he did. Therefore the suicide note is a fake.

"Up to this time, d'ye see, we have had a suicide which everybody thought was murder. Now we have a murder which everybody is going to take for suicide. We are going places and seeing things. All roads lead to the lunatic asylum. Can you by any chance oblige me with an idea?"

16

Alan shook his head.

"No ideas. I presume that the 'extra' thing which ailed Colin, and exercised Dr Grant so much, was carbon-dioxide poisoning?"

Dr Fell grunted assent. Fishing out the meerschaum pipe again, he filled and lighted it.

"Which," he assented, speaking between puffs like the Spirit of the Volcano, "leads us at full tide into our troubles. We can't blame Angus for that. The death box didn't load itself again with artificial ice.

"Somebody – who knew Colin was going to sleep there – set the trap again in a box already conveniently left under the bed. Somebody, who knew Colin's every movement, could nip up there ahead of him. He was drunk and wouldn't bother to investigate the box. All that saved his life was the fact that he slept with the window open, and roused himself in time. Query: who did that, and why?

"Final query: who killed Alec Forbes, and how, and why?"

Alan continued to shake his head doubtfully.

"You're still not convinced that Forbes's death was murder, my lad?"

"Frankly, I'm not. I still don't see why Forbes couldn't have killed both the others, or thought he had, and then killed himself."

"Logic? Or wishful thinking?"

Alan was honest. "A little of both, maybe. Aside from the money question, I should hate to think that Angus was such an old swine as to try to get an innocent man hanged."

"Angus," returned Dr Fell, "was neither an old swine nor an honest Christian gentleman. He was a realist who saw only one way to provide for those he was fond of. I do not defend it. But can you dare say you don't understand it?"

"It isn't that. I can't understand, either, why he took the blackout down from the window if he wanted to be sure of smothering himself with the . . ."

Alan paused, for the sudden expression which had come over Dr Fell's face was remarkable for its sheer idiocy. Dr Fell stared, and his eyes rolled. The pipe almost dropped from his mouth.

"O Lord! O Bacchus! O my ancient hat!" he breathed. "Blackout!"

"What is it?"

"The murderer's first mistake," said Dr Fell. "Come with me."

Hurriedly he swung round and blundered back into the hut again. Alan followed him, not without an effort. Dr Fell began a hurried search of the room. With an exclamation of triumph he found on the floor near the bed a piece of tar paper nailed to a light wooden frame. He held this up to the window, and it fitted.

"We ourselves can testify," he went on, with extraordinary intensity, "that when we arrived here there was no blackout on this window. Hey?"

"That's right."

"Yet the lamp" – he pointed –" had obviously been burning for a long time, far into the night. We can smell the odor of burned paraffin oil strongly even yet?"

"Yes."

Dr Fell stared into vacancy.

"Every inch of this neighborhood is patrolled all night by the Home Guard. A hurricane lantern gives a strong light. There wasn't even so much as a curtain, let alone a blackout, on this window when we arrived. How is it that nobody noticed that light?"

There was a pause.

"Maybe they just didn't see it."

"My dear chap! So much as a chink of light in these hills would draw down the Home Guard for miles round. No, no, no! That won't do."

"Well, maybe Forbes – before he hanged himself – blew out the lantern and took down the blackout. The window's open, we notice. Though I don't see why he should have done that."

Again Dr Fell shook his head with vehemence.

"I quote you again the habits of suicides. A suicide will never take his own life in darkness if there is any means of providing light. I do not analyze the psychology: I merely state the fact. Besides, Forbes wouldn't have been able to see to make all his preparations in the dark. No, no, no! It's fantastic!"

"What do you suggest, then?"

Dr Fell put his hands to his forehead. For a time he remained motionless, wheezing gently.

"I suggest," he replied, lowering his hands after an interval, "that, after Forbes had been murdered and strung up, the murderer himself extinguished the lantern. He poured out the oil remaining in it so that it should later seem to have burned itself out. Then he took down the blackout."

"But why in blazes bother to do that? Why not leave the blackout where it was, and go away, and leave the lantern to burn itself out?"

"Obviously because he had to make use of the window in making his escape."

This was the last straw.

"Look here," Alan said, with a sort of wild patience. He strode across. "Look at the damned window! It's covered by a steel grating nailed up solidly on the inside! Can you suggest any way, any way at all, by which a murderer could slide out through that?"

"Well – no. Not at the moment. And yet it was done."

They looked at each other.

From some distance away they heard the sound of a man's voice earnestly hallooing, and scraps of distant talk. They hurried to the door.

Charles Swan and Alistair Duncan were striding toward them. The lawyer, in a raincoat and bowler hat, appeared more cadaverous than ever; but his whole personality was suffused with a kind of dry triumph.

"I think you're a good deal of a cheap skate," Swan accused Alan, "to run away like that after you'd promised me all the news there was. If I hadn't had my car I'd have been stranded."

Duncan silenced him. Duncan's mouth had a grim, pleased curve. He bowed slightly to Dr Fell.

"Gentlemen," he said, taking up a position like a schoolmaster, "we have just learned from Dr Grant that Colin Campbell is suffering from the effects of carbonic acid gas."

"True," agreed Dr Fell.

"Administered probably from artificial ice taken from Angus Campbell's laboratory."

Again Dr Fell nodded.

"Can we therefore," pursued Duncan, putting his hands together and rubbing them softly, "have any doubts of how Angus died? Or of who administered the gas to him?"

"We cannot. If you'd care to glance in that cottage there," said Dr Fell, nodding toward it, "you will see the final proof which completes your case."

Duncan stepped quickly to the door, and just as quickly stepped back again. Swan, more determined or more callous, uttered an exclamation and went in.

There was a long silence while the lawyer seemed to be

screwing up his courage. His Adam's apple worked in his long throat above the too-large collar. He removed his bowler hat and wiped his forehead with a handkerchief. Then, replacing the hat and straightening his shoulders, he forced himself to follow Swan into the cottage.

Both of them reappeared, hastily and without dignity, pursued by a series of savage growls which rose to a yelping snarl. The dog, red-eyed, watched them from the doorway.

"Nice doggie!" crooned Duncan, with a leer of such patent hypocrisy that the dog snarled again.

"You shouldn't have touched him," said Swan. "The pooch naturally got sore. I want a telephone. Cripes, what a scoop!"

Duncan readjusted his ruffled dignity.

"So it *was* Alec Forbes," he said.

Dr Fell inclined his head.

"My dear sir," continued the lawyer, coming over to wring Dr Fell's hand with some animation, "I – we – can't thank you too much! I daresay you guessed, from the trade magazines and bills you borrowed from Angus's room, what had been used to kill him?"

"Yes."

"I cannot imagine," said Duncan, "why it was not apparent to all of us from the first. Though, of course, the effects of the gas had cleared away when Angus was found. No wonder the clasps of the dog carrier were closed! When I think how we imagined snakes and spiders and heaven knows what, I am almost amused. The whole thing is so extraordinarily simple, once you have grasped the design behind it."

"I agree," said Dr Fell. "By thunder, but I agree!"

"You – ah – observed the suicide note?"

"I did."

Duncan nodded with satisfaction.

"The insurance companies will have to eat their words now. There can be no question as to their paying in full."

Yet Duncan hesitated. Honesty evidently compelled him to worry at another point.

"There is just one thing, however, that I cannot quite understand. If Forbes placed the dog carrier under the bed before being ejected, as this gentleman" – he looked at Alan – "so intelligently suggested on Monday, how is it that Elspat and Kirstie did not observe it when they looked there?"

"Haven't you forgotten?" asked Dr Fell. "She *did* see it, as she has since told us. Miss Elspat Campbell's mind is as literal as a German's. You asked her whether there was a suitcase there, and she said no. That is all."

It would not be true to say that the worry cleared away altogether from Duncan's face. But he cheered up, although he gave Dr Fell a very curious look.

"You think the insurance companies will accept that correction?"

"I know the police will accept it. So the insurance companies will have to, whether they like it or not."

"A plain case?"

"A plain case."

"So it seems to me." Duncan cheered up still more. "Well, we must finish up this sad business as soon as we can. Have you informed the police about – this?"

"Miss Kathryn Campbell has gone to do so. She should be back at any minute. We had to break the door in, as you see, but we haven't touched anything else. After all, we don't want to be held as accessories after the fact."

Duncan laughed.

"You could hardly be held for that in any case. In Scots law, there is no such thing as an accessory after the fact."

"Is that so, now?" mused Dr Fell. He took the pipe out of his mouth and added abruptly: "Mr Duncan, were you ever acquainted with Robert Campbell?"

There was something in his words so arresting, even if so

inexplicable, that everyone turned to look at him. The faint thunder of the Falls of Coe appeared loud in the hush that followed.

"Robert?" repeated Duncan. "The third of the brothers?"

"Yes."

An expression of fastidious distaste crossed the lawyer's face. "Really, sir, to rake up old scandals –"

"Did you know him?" insisted Dr Fell.

"I did."

"What can you tell me about him? All I've learned so far is that he got into trouble and had to leave the country. What did he do? Where did he go? Above all, what was he like?"

Duncan grudgingly considered this.

"I knew him as a young man." He shot Dr Fell a quick glance. "Robert, if I may say so, was by far the cleverest and brainiest of his family. But he had a streak of bad blood: which, fortunately, missed both Angus and Colin. He had trouble at the bank where he worked. Then there was a shooting affray over a barmaid.

"As to where he is now, I can't say. He went abroad – the colonies, America – I don't know where, because he slipped aboard a ship at Glasgow. You surely cannot consider that the matter is of any importance now?"

"No. I daresay not."

His attention was diverted. Kathryn Campbell scrambled down the bank, crossed the stream, and came toward them.

"I've got in touch with the police," she reported breathlessly, after a sharp glance at Duncan and Swan. "There's a hotel, the Glencoe Hotel, at the village of Glencoe about two miles farther on. The telephone number is Ballachulish – pronounced Ballahoolish – four-five."

"Did you talk to Inspector Donaldson?"

"Yes. He says he's always known Alec Forbes would do something like this. He says we needn't wait here, if we don't want to."

Her eyes strayed toward the cottage, and moved away uneasily.

"Please. *Must* you stay here? Couldn't we go on to the hotel and have something to eat? I ask because the proprietress knew Mr Forbes very well."

Dr Fell stirred with interest.

"So?"

"Yes. She says he was a famous cyclist. She says he could cover incredible distances at incredible speeds, in spite of the amount he drank."

Duncan uttered a soft exclamation. With a significant gesture to the others, he went round the side of the cottage, and they instinctively followed him. Behind the cottage was an outhouse, against which leaned a racing bicycle fitted out with a luggage grid at the back. Duncan pointed to it.

"The last link, gentlemen. It explains how Forbes could have got from here to Inveraray and back whenever he liked. Did your informant add anything else, Miss Campbell?"

"Not much. She said he came up here to drink and fish and work out schemes for perpetual motion, and things of that sort. She said the last time she saw him was yesterday, in the bar of the hotel. They practically had to throw him out at closing time in the afternoon. She says he was a bad man, who hated everything and everybody but animals."

Dr Fell slowly walked forward and put his hand on the handlebar of the bicycle. Alan saw, with uneasiness, there was again on his face the startled expression, the wandering blankness of idiocy, which he had seen there once before. This time it was deeper and more explosive.

"O Lord!" thundered Dr Fell, whirling round as though galvanized. "What a turnip I've been! What a remarkable donkey! What a thundering dunce!"

"Without," observed Duncan, "without sharing the views you express, may I ask why you express them?"

Dr Fell turned to Kathryn.

"You're quite right," he said seriously, after reflecting for a time. "We must get on to that hotel. Not only to refresh the inner man; though I, to be candid, am ravenous. But I want to use a telephone. I want to use a telephone like billy-o. There's a million-to-one chance against it, of course; but the million-to-one chance came off before and it may happen again."

"What million-to-one chance?" asked Duncan, not without exasperation. "To whom do you want to telephone?"

"To the local commandant of the Home Guard," answered Dr Fell, and lumbered round the side of the cottage with his cloak flying out behind him.

17

"Alan," Kathryn asked, "Alec Forbes didn't really kill himself, did he?"

It was late at night and raining. They had drawn up their chairs before a brightly burning wood fire in the sitting-room at Shira.

Alan was turning over the pages of a family album, with thick padded covers and gilt-topped leaves. For some time Kathryn had been silent, her elbow on the arm of the chair and her chin in her hand, staring into the fire. She dropped the question out of nowhere: flatly, as her habit was.

He did not raise his eyes.

"Why is it," he said, "that photographs taken some years ago are always so hilariously funny? You can take down anybody's family album and split your sides. If it happens to contain pictures of somebody you know, the effect is even more pronounced. Why? Is it the clothes, or the expressions, or what? We weren't really as funny as that, were we?"

Disregarding her, he turned over a page or two.

"The women, as a rule, come out better than the men. Here is one of Colin as a young man, which looks as though he'd drunk about a quart of the Doom of the Campbells before leering at the photographer. Aunt Elspat, on the other hand, was a really fine-looking woman. Bold-eyed brunette; Mrs Siddons touch. Here she is in a man's Highland costume: bonnet, feather, plaid, and all."

"Alan Campbell!"

"Angus, on the other hand, always tried to look so dignified and pensive that –"

"Alan darling."

He sat up with a snap. The rain pattered against the windows.

"What did you say?" he demanded.

"It was only a manner of speaking." She elevated her chin. "Or at least – well, anyway, I *had* to get your attention somehow. Alec Forbes didn't really kill himself, did he?"

"What makes you think that?"

"I can see it in the way you look," returned Kathryn; and he had an uncomfortable feeling that she would always be able to do this, which would provide some critical moments in the future.

"Besides," she went on, peering round to make sure they were not overheard, and lowering her voice, "why should he? He certainly couldn't have been the one who tried to kill poor Colin."

Reluctantly Alan closed the album.

The memory of the day stretched out behind him: the meal at the Glencoe Hotel, the endless repetitions by Alistair Duncan of how Alec Forbes had committed his crimes and then hanged himself, all the while that Dr Fell said nothing, and Kathryn brooded, and Swan sent off to the *Daily Floodlight* a story which he described as a honey.

"And why," he asked, "couldn't Forbes have tried to kill Colin?"

"Because he couldn't have known Colin was sleeping in the tower room."

(Damn! So she's spotted that!)

"Didn't you hear what the proprietress of the hotel said?" Kathryn insisted. "Forbes was in the bar of the hotel until closing time yesterday afternoon. Well, it was early in the afternoon here that Colin swore his great oath to sleep in the tower. How on earth could Forbes have known that? It was a snap decision which Colin made on the spur of the moment, and couldn't have been known outside the house."

Alan hesitated.

Kathryn lowered her voice still further.

"Oh, I'm not going to broadcast it! Alan, I know what Dr Fell thinks. As he told us going out to the car, he thinks Angus committed suicide. Which is horrible, and yet I believe it. I believe it still more now that we've heard about the artificial ice."

She shivered.

"At least, we do know it isn't – supernatural. When we were thinking about snakes and spiders and ghosts and whatnots, I tell you I was frightened out of my wits. And all the while it was nothing but a lump of dry ice!"

"Most terrors are like that."

"Are they? Who played ghost, then? And who killed Forbes?"

Alan brooded. "*If* Forbes was murdered," he said, half-conceding this for the first time, "the motive for it is clear. It was to prove Angus's death was murder after all, like the attempt on Colin; to saddle Forbes with both crimes; and to clean up the whole business."

"To get the insurance money?"

"That's what it looks like."

The rain pattered steadily. Kathryn gave a quick glance at the door to the hall.

"But, Alan! In that case . . . ?"

"Yes. I know what you're thinking."

"And, in any case, how *could* Forbes have been murdered?"

"Your guess is as good as mine. Dr Fell thinks the murderer got out by way of the window. Yes, I know the window was covered with an untouched grating! But so was the end of the dog carrier, if you remember. Twenty-four hours ago I would have sworn nothing could have got out of the dog carrier grating, either. And yet something did."

He broke off, with an air of elaborate casualness and a warning glance to Kathryn, as they heard footsteps in the hall. He was again turning over the pages of the album when Swan came into the sitting-room.

Swan was almost as wet as he had been after Elspat's two pails of water. He stamped up to the fire, and let his hands drip into it.

"If I don't catch pneumonia one way or the other, before this thing is over," he announced, shifting from one foot to the other, "the reason won't be for want of bad luck. I've been obeying orders and trying to stick to Dr Fell. You'd think that would be easy, wouldn't you?"

"Yes."

Swan's face was bitter.

"Well, it isn't. He's ditched me twice today. He's doing something with the Home Guard. Or at least he was before this rain started in. But what it is I can't find out and Sherlock Holmes himself couldn't guess. Anything up?"

"No. We were just looking at family portraits." Alan turned over pages. He passed one photograph, started to turn the page, and then, with sudden interest, went back to it. "Hullo," he said. "I've seen *that* face somewhere!"

It was a full-face view of a light-haired man with a heavy down-curved mustache, *circa* 1906, a handsome face with washed-out eyes. This impression, however, may have come from the faded brown color of the photograph. Across the lower right-hand corner was written in faded ink, with curlicues, "Best of luck!"

"Of course you've seen it," said Kathryn. "It's a Campbell. There's resemblance, more or less, in every one of our particular crowd."

"No, no. I mean –"

He detached the photograph from the four slits in the cardboard, and turned it over. Across the back was written in the same handwriting, "Robert Campbell, July, '05."

"So that's the brainy Robert!"

Swan, who had been peering over his shoulder, was clearly interested in something else.

"Wait a minute!" Swan urged, fitting back the photograph again and turning back a page quickly. "Cripes, what a beauty! Who's the good-looking woman?"

"That's Aunt Elspat."

"*Who?*"

"Elspat Campbell."

Swan winked his eyes. "Not the old hag who – who –" Wordlessly, his hands went to his new suit, and his face became distorted.

"Yes. The same one who baptized you. Look at this other of her in Highland costume, where she shows her legs. If I may mention the subject, they are very fine legs; though maybe on the heavy and muscular side for popular taste nowadays."

Kathryn could not restrain herself.

"But nothing, of course," she sneered, "to compare to the legs of your precious Duchess of Cleveland."

Swan begged their attention.

"Look," he said impressively, "I don't want to seem inquisitive. But –" his voice acquired a note of passion – "who *is* this dame from Cleveland, anyhow? Who is Charles? Who is Russell? And how did you get tangled up with her? I know I oughtn't to ask; but I can't sleep nights for thinking about it."

"The Duchess of Cleveland," said Alan, "was Charles's mistress."

"Yes, I gathered that. But is she your mistress too?"

"No. And she didn't come from Cleveland, Ohio, because she's been dead for more than two hundred years."

Swan stared at him.

"You're kidding me."

"I am not. We were having a historical argument, and –"

"I tell you, you're kidding me!" repeated Swan, with something like incredulous horror in his voice. "There's *got* to be a real Cleveland woman in it! As I said about you in my first story to the *Floodlight* –"

He paused. He opened his mouth, and shut it again. He seemed to feel that he had made a slip; as, in fact, he had. Two pairs of eyes fastened on him during an ominous silence.

"What," Kathryn asked very clearly, "what did you say about us in your first story to the *Floodlight?*"

"Nothing at all. Word of honor, I didn't! Just a little joke, nothing libelous in it at all –"

"Alan," murmured Kathryn, with her eye on a corner of the ceiling, "don't you think you'd better get down the claymores again?"

Swan had instinctively moved away until his back was shielded against the wall. He spoke in deep earnest.

"After all, you're going to get married! I overheard Dr Fell himself say you had to get married. So what's wrong? I didn't mean any harm." (And clearly, thought Alan, he hadn't.) "I only said –"

"What a pity," continued Kathryn, still with her eye on the ceiling, "what a pity Colin hasn't got the use of his legs. But I hear he's a rare hand with a shotgun. And, since his bedroom windows face the main road –"

She paused, significantly musing, as Kirstie MacTavish flung open the door.

"Colin Campbell wants tae see you," she announced in her soft, sweet voice.

Swan changed color.

"He wants to see who?"

"He wants tae see all o' you."

"But he isn't allowed visitors, is he?" cried Kathryn.

"I dinna ken. He's drinkin' whusky in bed, annahoo."

"Well, Mr Swan," said Kathryn, folding her arms, "after giving us a solemn promise, which you promptly broke and intended to break; after accepting hospitality here under false pretenses; after being handed on a plate probably the only good story you ever got in your life; and hoping to get some more – have you the courage to go up and face Colin now?"

"But you've got to look at my side of it, Miss Campbell!"

"Oh?"

"Colin Campbell'll understand! He's a good egg! He . . ." As an idea evidently occurred to him, Swan turned to the maid. "Look. He's not pickled, is he?"

"Wha'?"

"Pickled. Soused," said Swan apprehensively, "cockeyed. Plastered. Full."

Kirstie was enlightened. She assured him that Colin was not full. Though the effectiveness of this assurance was somewhat modified by Kirstie's experienced belief that no man is full until he can fall down two successive flights of stairs without injury, Swan did not know this and it served its purpose.

"I'll put it up to him," Swan argued with great earnestness. "And in the meantime I'll put it up to both of you. I come up here; and what happens to me?"

"Not a patch," said Kathryn, "on what's going to happen. But go on."

Swan did not hear her.

"I get chased along a road," he continued, "and get a serious injury that might have given me blood-poisoning. All right. I come round the next day, in a brand-new suit that cost ten guineas at Austin Reed's, and that mad woman empties two buckets of water over me. Not *one* bucket, mind you. *Two*."

"Alan Campbell," said Kathryn fiercely, "do you find anything so very funny in this?"

Alan could not help himself. He was leaning back and roaring.

"Alan Campbell!"

"I can't help it," protested Alan, wiping the tears out of his eyes. "It just occurs to me that you'll have to marry me after all."

"Can I announce that?" asked Swan instantly.

"Alan Campbell, what on earth do you mean? I'll do no such thing! The idea!"

"You can't help yourself, my wench. It's the only solution to our difficulties. I have not yet read the *Daily Floodlight*, but I have my suspicions as to the nature of the hints that will have appeared there."

Swan seized on this.

"I knew you wouldn't be sore," he said, his face lighting up. "There's nothing anybody could object to, I swear! I never said a word about your always going to bawdy-houses. That's really libelous anyway –"

"What this," inquired Kathryn, breaking off with some quickness, "about you going to bawdy houses?"

"I'm sorry I said that," interposed Swan, with equal quickness. "I wouldn't have said it for the world in front of you, Miss Campbell, only it slipped out. It probably isn't true anyway, so just forget it. All I wanted to say was that I've got to play the game straight both with you and the public."

"Are ye comin'?" asked Kirstie, still waiting patiently in the doorway.

Swan straightened his tie.

"Yes, we are. And I know Colin Campbell, who's as good an egg as ever walked, will understand my position."

"I hope he does," breathed Kathryn. "Oh, good heavens, I hope he does! You did say he'd got some whisky up there, didn't you, Kirstie?"

It was, in a sense, unnecessary to answer this question. As the three of them followed Kirstie up the stairs, and along the hall to the back of the house, it was answered by Colin himself. The doors at Shira were good thick doors, and very little in the nature of noise could penetrate far through them. The voice they heard, therefore, was not very loud. But it carried distinctly to the head of the stairs.

> *"I love a lassie, a boh-ny, boh-ny lassie;*
> *She's as puir as the li-ly in the dell!*
> *She's as sweet as the heather, the boh-ny pur-ple heath-er –"*

The singing stopped abruptly as Kirstie opened the door. In a spacious back bedroom with oak furniture, Colin Campbell lay on what should have been, and undoubtedly was, a bed of pain. But you would never have guessed this from the demeanor of the tough old sinner.

His body was bandaged from the waist down, one leg supported a little above the level of the bed by a portable iron framework and supports. But his back was hunched into pillows in such a way that he could just raise his head.

Though his hair, beard, and mustache had been trimmed, he managed to look shaggier than ever. Out of this, fiercely affable eyes peered from a flushed face. The airless room smelled like a distillery.

Colin had insisted, as an invalid, on having plenty of light, and the chandelier glowed with bulbs. They illuminated his truculent grin, his gaudy pajama tops, and the untidy litter of articles on the bedside table. His bed was drawn up by one blacked-out window.

"Come in!" he shouted. "Come in, and keep the old crock company. Filthy position to be in. Kirstie, go and fetch three more glasses and another decanter. You! The rest of you! Pull up your chairs. Here, where I can see you. I've got nothing to do but this."

He was dividing his attention between the decanter, somewhat depleted, and a very light 20-bore shotgun, which he was attempting to clean and oil.

18

"Kitty-kat my dear, it's a pleasure to see your face," he continued, holding up the gun so that he could look at her through one of the barrels. "What have you been up to now? I say. Would you like to point out something to me, so that I could have a shot at it?"

Swan took one look at him, turned round, and made a beeline for the door.

Kathryn instantly turned the key in the lock, and held tightly to it as she backed away.

"Indeed I would, Uncle Colin," said Kathryn sweetly.

"That's my Kitty-kat. And how are you, Alan? And you, Horace Greeley: how are *you*? I'm filthy, I don't mind telling you. Swaddled up like a blooming Chinese woman, though they've got more of me than just my feet. God's wounds! If they'd only give me a *chair*, I could at least move about."

He reflected.

Snapping shut the breech of the shotgun, he lowered it to stand against the side of the bed.

"I'm happy," he added abruptly. "Maybe I shouldn't be, but I am. You've heard, haven't you, about what happened to me? Artificial ice. Same as Angus. It was murder, after all. It's a pity about poor old Alec Forbes, though. I never did dislike the fellow. Stop a bit. Where's Fell? Why isn't Fell here? What have you done with Fell?"

Kathryn was grimly determined.

"He's out with the Home Guard, Uncle Colin. Listen. There's something we've got to tell you. This wretch of a reporter, after promising –"

"What the devil does he want to go joining the Home Guard for, at *his* age and weight? They may not pot him for a parachutist; but if they see him against the skyline they'll ruddy well pot him for a parachute. It's crazy. It's worse than that: it's downright dangerous."

"Uncle Colin, *will* you listen to me, please?"

"Yes, my dear, of course. Joining the Home Guard! Never heard such nonsense in my life!"

"This reporter –"

"He didn't say anything about it when he was in here awhile ago. All he wanted to do was ask a lot of questions about poor old Rabbie; and what we'd all been saying up in the tower room on Monday. Besides, how could he get into the Home Guard in Scotland? Are you pulling my leg?"

Kathryn's expression was by this time so desperate that even Colin noticed it. He broke off, peering shaggily at her.

"Nothing wrong, is there, Kitty-kat?"

"Yes, there is. That is, if you'd just listen to me for a moment! Do you remember that Mr Swan promised not to say a word about anything that happened here, if we let him get what stories he wanted?"

Colin's eyebrows drew together.

"God's wounds! You didn't print in that rag of yours that we stuck you in the seat of the pants with a claymore?"

"No, so help me I didn't!" returned Swan, instantly and with patent truth. "I didn't say a word about it. I've got the paper, and I can prove it."

"Then what's biting you, Kitty-kat?"

"He's said, or intimated, dreadful things about Alan and me. I don't know exactly what; and Alan doesn't even seem to care; but it's something about Alan and me being immoral together –"

Colin stared at her. Then he leaned back and bellowed with laughter. The mirth brought tears into his eyes.

"Well, aren't you?"

"No! Just because of a dreadful accident, just because we *had* to spend the night in the same compartment on the train from London –"

"You didn't have to spend the night in the same room here on Monday," Colin pointed out. "But you ruddy well did. Eh?"

"They spent the night in the same room here?" Swan demanded quickly.

"Of course they did," roared Colin. "Come on, Kitty-kat! Be a man! I mean, be a woman! Admit it! Have the courage of your convictions. What were you doing, then, if you weren't improving your time? Nonsense!"

"You see, Miss Campbell," pleaded Swan, "I had to get the sex-angle into the story somehow, and that was the only way to do it. *He* understands. Your boy-friend understands. There's nothing at all to worry about, not the least little thing."

Kathryn looked from one to the other of them. An expression of hopeless despair went over her pink face. Tears came into her eyes, and she sat down in a chair and put her face in her hands.

"Here! Easy!" said Alan. "I've just been pointing out to her, Colin, that her reputation is hopelessly compromised unless she marries me now. I asked her to marry me –"

"You never did."

"Well, I do so now, in front of witnesses. Miss Campbell: will you do me the honor of becoming my wife?"

Kathryn raised a tearstained face of exasperation.

"Of course I will, you idiot!" she stormed at him. "But why couldn't you do it decently, as I've given you a hundred

179

opportunities to, instead of blackmailing me into it? Or saying I blackmailed you into it?"

Colin's eyes opened wide.

"Do you mean," he bellowed delightedly, "there's going to be a wedding?"

"Can I print that?"

"Yes to both questions," replied Alan.

"My dear Kitty-kat! My dear fellow! By George!" said Colin, rubbing his hands. "This calls for such a celebration as these walls haven't seen since the night Elspat's virtue fell in 1900. Where's Kirstie with that decanter? God's wounds! I wonder if there are any bagpipes in the house? I haven't tried 'em for years, but what I could do once would warm the cockles of your heart."

"You're not mad at *me*?" asked Swan anxiously.

"At you? Great Scott, no! Why should I be? Come over here, old chap, and sit down!"

"Then what," persisted Swan, "did you want that toy shotgun for?"

"'Toy' shotgun, is it? 'Toy' shotgun?" Colin snatched up the 20-bore. "Do you know it takes a devil of a lot more skill and accuracy to use this than it does a 12-bore? Don't believe that, eh? Like me to show you?"

"No, no, no. I'll take your word for it!"

"That's better. Come and have a drink. No, we haven't got any glasses. Where's Kirstie? And Elspat! We've got to have Elspat here. Elspat!"

Kathryn was compelled to unlock the door. Swan, with an expiring sigh of relief, sat down and stretched his legs like one completely at home. He sprang up again with deep suspicion when Elspat appeared.

Elspat, however, ignored him with such icy pointedness that he backed away. Elspat gave them each in turn, except Swan, an unfathomable glance. Her eyelids were puffed and reddish, and her mouth was a straight line. Alan tried to see in her some resemblance to the handsome woman of the old photograph; but it was gone, all gone.

"Look here, old girl," said Colin. He stretched out his hand to her. "I've got great news. Glorious news. These two" – he pointed –" are going to get married."

Elspat did not say anything. Her eyes rested on Alan, studying him. Then they moved to Kathryn, studying her for a long time. She went over to Kathryn, and quickly kissed her on the cheek. Two tears, amazing tears, overflowed Elspat's eyes.

"Here, I say!" Colin stirred uncomfortably. Then he glared. "It's the same old family custom," he complained in a querulous voice. "Always turn on the waterworks when there's going to be a wedding. This is a *happy* occasion, hang it! Stop that!"

Elspat still remained motionless. Her face worked.

"If you don't stop that, I'm going to throw something," yelled Colin. "Can't you say, 'Congratulations,' or anything like that? Have we got any pipes in the house, by the way?"

"Ye'll hae no godless merriment here, Colin Campbell," snapped Elspat, choking out the words despite her working face. She fought back by instinct, while Alan's discomfort increased.

"Aye, I'll gie ye ma blessin'," she said, looking first at Kathryn and then at Alan. "If the blessin' of an auld snaggletooth body's worth a groat tae ye."

"Well, then," said Colin sulkily, "we can at least have the whisky. You'll drink their health, I hope?"

"Aye. I caud du wi' that tonight. The de'il's walkin' on ma grave." She shivered.

"I never saw such a lot of killjoys in all my born days," grumbled Colin. But he brightened as Kirstie brought in the glasses and a decanter.

"One more glass, my wench. Stop a bit. Maybe we'd better have a third decanter, eh?"

"Just a moment!" said Alan. He looked round at them and,

in some uneasiness, at the shotgun. "You're not proposing another binge tonight, are you?"

"Binge! Nonsense!" said Colin, pouring himself a short one evidently to give him strength to pour for the others, and gulping it down. "Who said anything about a binge? We're drinking health and happiness to the bride, that's all. You can't object to that, can you?"

"*I* can't," smiled Kathryn.

"Nor me," observed Swan. "I feel grand!" Swan added. "I forgive everybody. I even forgive madam," – he hesitated, for he was clearly frightened of Elspat – "for ruining a suit that cost me ten guineas."

Colin spoke persuasively.

"See here, Elspat. I'm sorry about Angus. But there it is. And it's turned out for the best. If he had to die, I don't mind admitting it's got me out of a bad financial hole.

"Do you know what I'm going to do? No more doctoring in Manchester, for the moment. I'm going to get a ketch and go for a cruise in the South Seas. And you, Elspat. You can get a dozen big pictures painted of Angus, and look at 'em all day. Or you can go to London and see the jitterbugs. You're safe, old girl."

Elspat's face was white.

"Aye," she blazed at him. "*And d'ye ken why we're safe?*"

"Steady!" cried Alan.

Even in his mist of good will and exhilaration, he knew what was coming. Kathryn knew too. They both made a move toward Elspat, but she paid no attention.

"I'll have ma conscience nae mair damned wi' lees. D'ye ken why we're safe?"

She whirled round to Swan. Addressing him for the first time, she announced calmly that Angus had killed himself; she poured out the entire story, with her reasons for believing it. And every word of it was true.

"Now that's very interesting, ma'am," said Swan, who had

taken one glass of whisky and was holding out his tumbler for a second. He appeared flattered by her attention. "Then you're not mad at me any longer either?"

Elspat stared at him.

"Mad at ye? Hoots! D'ye hear what I'm saying?"

"Yes, of course, ma'am," Swan replied soothingly. "And of course I understand how this thing has upset you –"

"Mon, dinna ye believe me?"

Swan threw back his head and laughed.

"I hate to contradict a lady, ma'am. But if you'll just have a word with the police, or with Dr Fell, or with these people here, you'll see that either somebody has been kidding you or you've been kidding yourself. I ought to know, oughtn't I? Hasn't anybody told you that Alec Forbes killed himself, and left a note admitting he killed Mr Campbell?"

Elspat drew in her breath. Her face wrinkled up. She turned and looked at Colin, who nodded.

"It's true, Elspat. Come abreast of the times! Where have you been all day?"

It stabbed Alan to the heart to see her. She groped over to a chair and sat down. A human being, a sentient, living, hurt human being, emerged from behind the angry clay in which Elspat set her face to the world.

"Ye're no' deceivin' me?" she insisted. "Ye swear to the Guid Man – !"

Then she began to swing back and forth in the rocking chair. She began to laugh, showing that she had fine teeth; and it kindled and illumined her face. Her whole being seemed to breathe a prayer.

Angus had not died in the sin of suicide. He had not gone to the bad place. And Elspat, this Elspat whose real surname nobody knew, rocked back and forth and laughed and was happy.

Colin Campbell, serenely missing all this, was still acting as barman.

"You understand," he beamed, "neither Fell nor I ever for a minute thought it *was* suicide. Still, it's just as well to get the whole thing tidied up. I never for a second thought you didn't know, or I'd have crawled off this bed to tell you. Now be a good sport. I know this is still officially a house of mourning. But, under the circumstances, what about getting me those pipes?"

Elspat got to her feet and went out of the room.

"By Jupiter," breathed Colin, "she's gone to get 'em! . . . What ails you, Kitty-kat?"

Kathryn regarded the door with uncertain, curiously shining eyes. She bit her lip. Her eyes moved over toward Alan.

"I don't know," she answered. "I'm happy" – here she glared at Alan – "and yet I feel all sort of funny and mixed up."

"Your English grammar," said Alan, "is abominable. But your sentiments are correct. That's what she believes now; and that's what Elspat has got to go on believing. Because, of course, it's true."

"Of course," agreed Kathryn quickly. "I wonder, Uncle Colin, whether you would do me a big favor?"

"Anything in the world, my dear."

"Well," said Kathryn, hesitantly extending the tumbler, "it isn't very much, perhaps; but would you mind making my drink just a *little* stronger?"

"Now that's my Kitty-kat!" roared Colin. "Here you are . . . Enough?"

"A little more, please."

"A little *more?*"

"Yes, please."

"Cripes," muttered Swan, on whom the first smashing, shuddering effect of the Doom of the Campbells had now passed to a quickened speech and excitement, "you two professors are teamed up right. I don't understand how you do it. Does anybody, maybe, now, feel like a song?"

Beatific with his head among the pillows, as though

enthroned in state, Colin lifted the shotgun and waved it in the air as though conducting an orchestra. His bass voice beat against the windows.

"I love a lassie, a boh-ny, boh-ny las-sie –"

Swan, drawing his chin far into his collar, assumed an air of solemn portentousness. Finding the right pitch after a preliminary cough, he moved his glass gently in time and joined in.

"She's as pure as the li-ly in the dell – !"

To Alan, lifting his glass in a toast to Kathryn, there came a feeling that all things happened for the best; and that tomorrow could take care of itself. The exhilaration of being in love, the exhilaration of merely watching Kathryn, joined with the exhilaration of the potent brew in his hand. He smiled at Kathryn; she smiled back; and they both joined in.

"She's as sweet as the heath-er, the boh-ny pur-ple heather –"

He had a good loud baritone, and Kathryn a fairly audible soprano. Their quartet made the room ring. To Aunt Elspat, returning with a set of bagpipes – which she grimly handed to Colin, and which he eagerly seized without breaking off the song – it must have seemed that old days had returned.

"A'weel," said Aunt Elspat resignedly. "A'weel!"

19

Alan Campbell opened one eye.

From somewhere in remote distances, muffled beyond sight or sound, his soul crawled back painfully, through subterranean corridors, up into his body again. Toward the last it moved to the conviction that he was looking at a family photograph album, from which there stared back at him a face he had seen, somewhere, only today . . .

Then he was awake.

The first eye was bad enough. But, when he opened the second eye, such a rush of anguish flowed through his brain that he knew what was wrong with him, and realized fairly that he had done it again.

He lay back and stared at the cracks on the ceiling. There was sunlight in the room.

He had a violent headache, and his throat was dry. But it occurred to him in a startled sort of way that he did not feel nearly as bad as he had felt the first time. This prompted an uneasy flash of doubt. Did the infernal stuff take hold of you? Was it (as the temperance tracts said) an insidious poison whose effects seemed to grow less day by day?

Then another feeling, heartening or disheartening according to how you viewed the stuff, took possession of him.

When he searched his memory he could recall nothing except blurred scenes which seemed to be dominated by the noise of bagpipes, and a vision of Elspat swinging back and forth beatifically in a rocking chair amidst it.

Yet no sense of sin oppressed him, no sense of guilt or enormity. He *knew* that his conduct had been such as becomes a gentleman even *en pantoufles*. It was a strange conviction, but a real one. He did not even quail when Kathryn opened the door.

On the contrary, this morning it was Kathryn who appeared guilty and hunted. On the tray she carried not one cup of black coffee, but two. She put the tray on the bedside table, and looked at him.

"It ought to be you," she said, after clearing her throat, "who brought this to me this morning. But I knew you'd be disgusting and sleep past noon. I suppose you don't remember anything about last night either?"

He tried to sit up, easing the throb in his head.

"Well, no. Er – I wasn't – ?"

"No, you were not. Alan Campbell, there never was such a stuffed shirt as you who ever lived. You just sat and beamed as though you owned the earth. But you *will* quote poetry. When you began on Tennyson, I feared the worst. You recited the whole of 'The Princess,' and nearly all of 'Maud.' When you actually had the face to quote that bit about, 'Put thy sweet hand in mine and trust in me,' and patted my hand as you did it – well, really!"

Averting his eyes, he reached after the coffee.

"I wasn't aware I knew so much Tennyson."

"You didn't, really. But when you couldn't remember, you just thought for a moment, and then said, 'Umble-bumble, umble-bumble,' and went on."

"Never mind. At least, we were all right?"

Kathryn lowered the cup she had raised to her lips. The cup rattled and clicked on its saucer.

"All right?" she repeated with widening eyes. "When that wretch Swan is probably in a hospital now?"

Alan's head gave a violent throb.

"We didn't – ?"

"No, not you. Uncle Colin."

"My God, he didn't assault Swan again? But they're great pals! He couldn't have assaulted Swan again! What happened?"

"Well, it was all right until Colin had about his fifteenth Doom; and Swan, who was also what he called 'canned' and a little too cocksure, brought out the newspaper article he wrote yesterday. He'd smuggled the paper in in case we didn't like it."

"Yes?"

"It wasn't so bad, really. I admit that. Everything was all right until Swan described how Colin had decided to sleep in the tower-room."

"Yes?"

"Swan's version of the incident ran something like this. You remember, he was hanging about outside the sitting-room windows? His story said: 'Dr Colin Campbell, a deeply religious man, placed his hand on the Bible and swore an oath that he would not enter the church again until the family ghost had ceased to walk in the melancholy Castle of Shira.' For about ten seconds Colin just looked at him. Then he pointed to the door and said, 'Out.' Swan didn't understand until Colin turned completely purple and said, 'Out of this house and stay out.' Colin grabbed his shotgun, and –"

"He didn't – ?"

"Not just then. But when Swan leaped downstairs, Colin said, 'Turn out the light and take down the blackout. I want to get him from the window as he goes up the road.' His bed is by the window, you remember."

"You don't mean to say Colin shot Swan in the seat of the pants as he ran for Inveraray?"

"No," answered Kathryn, "Colin didn't. *I* did."

189

Her voice became a wail.

"Alan darling, we've *got* to get out of this insidious country! First you, and now me. I don't know what's come over me; I honestly don't!"

Alan's head was aching still harder.

"But wait a minute! Where was I? Didn't I interfere?"

"You didn't even notice. You were reciting 'Sir Galahad' to Elspat. The rain had cleared off – it was four o'clock in the morning – and the moon was up. I was boiling angry with Swan, you see. And there he was in the road.

"He must have heard the window go up, and seen the moonlight on the shotgun. Because he gave one look, and never ran so fast even on the Monday night. I said, 'Uncle Colin, let *me* have a go.' He said, 'All right; but let him get a sporting distance away; we don't want to hurt him.' Ordinarily I'm frightened of guns, and I couldn't have hit the side of a barn door. But that wretched stuff made everything different. I loosed off blindly, and got a bull's-eye with the second barrel.

"Alan, do you think he'll have me arrested? And don't you *dare* laugh, either!"

"'Pompilia, will you let them murder me?'" murmured Alan. He finished his coffee, propped himself upright, and steadied a swimming world. "Never mind," he said. "I'll go and smooth him down."

"But suppose I – ?"

Alan studied the forlorn figure.

"You couldn't have hurt him much. Not at a distance, with a twenty-bore and a light load. He didn't fall down, did he?"

"No; he only ran harder."

"Then it's all right."

"But what am I to *do*?"

"'Put thy sweet hand in mine and trust in me.'"

"Alan Campbell!"

"Well, isn't it the proper course?"

Kathryn sighed. She walked to the window, and looked down over the loch. Its waters were peaceful, agleam in sunshine.

"And that," she told him, after a pause, "isn't all."

"Not more – !"

"No, no, no! Not more trouble of that kind, anyway. I got the letter this morning. Alan, I've been recalled."

"Recalled?"

"From my holiday. By the college. A.R.P. I also saw this morning's Scottish *Daily Express*. It looks as though the real bombing is going to begin."

The sunlight was as fair, the hills as golden and purple, as ever. Alan took a packet of cigarettes from the bedside table. He lit one and inhaled smoke. Though it made his head swim, he sat contemplating the loch and smoking steadily.

"So our holiday," he said, "is a kind of entr'acte."

"Yes," said Kathryn, without turning round. "Alan, *do* you love me?"

"You know I do."

"Then do we care?"

"No."

There was a silence.

"When have you got to go?" he asked presently.

"Tonight, I'm afraid. That's what the letter says."

"Then," he declared briskly, "we can't waste any more time. The sooner I get my own things packed, the better. I hope we can get adjoining sleepers on the train. We've done all we can do here anyway, which wasn't much to start with. The case, officially, is closed. All the same – I should have liked to see the real end of it, if there is an end."

"You may see the end of it yet," Kathryn told him, and turned round from the window.

"Meaning what?"

She wrinkled up her forehead, and her nervous manner was not entirely due to her apprehensions about the night before.

"You see," she went on, "Dr Fell is here. When I told him I had to go back tonight, he said he had every reason to believe he would be going as well. I said, 'But what about you-know?' He said, 'You-know will, I think, take care of itself.' But he said it in a queer way that made me think there's something going on. Something – rather terrible. He didn't come back here until nearly dawn this morning. He wants to see you, by the way."

"I'll be dressed in half a tick. Where is everybody else this morning?"

"Colin's still asleep. Elspat, even Kirstie, are out. There's nobody here but you and me and Dr Fell. Alan, it isn't hangover and it isn't Swan and it isn't nerves. But – I'm frightened. Please come downstairs as quick as you can."

He told himself, when he nicked his face in shaving, that this was due to the brew of the night before. He told himself that his own apprehensions were caused by an upset stomach and the misadventures of Swan.

Shira was intensely quiet. Only the sun entered. When you turned on a tap, or turned it off, ghostly clankings went down through the house and shivered away. And, as Alan went down to get his breakfast, he saw Dr Fell in the sitting-room.

Dr Fell, in his old black alpaca suit and string tie, occupied the sofa. He was sitting in the warm, golden sunlight, the meerschaum pipe between his teeth, and his expression far away. He had the air of a man who meditates a dangerous business and is not quite sure of his course. The ridges of his waistcoat rose and fell with slow, gentle wheezings. His big mop of gray-streaked hair had fallen over one eye.

Alan and Kathryn shared buttered toast and more coffee. They did not speak much. Neither knew quite what to do. It was like the feeling of not knowing whether you had been summoned to the headmaster's study or hadn't.

But the question was solved for them.

"Good morning!" called a voice.

They hurried out into the hall.

Alistair Duncan, in an almost summery and skittish-looking brown suit, was standing at the open front door. He wore a soft hat and carried a briefcase. He raised his hand to the knocker of the open door as though by way of illustration.

"There did not seem to be anybody about," he said. His voice, though meant to be pleasant, had a faint irritated undertone.

Alan glanced to the right. Through the open door of the sitting-room he could see Dr Fell stir, grunt, and lift his head as though roused out of sleep. Alan looked back to the tall, stoop-shouldered figure of the lawyer, framed against the shimmering loch outside.

"*May* I come in?" inquired Duncan politely.

"P-please do," stammered Kathryn.

"Thank you." Duncan stepped in gingerly, removing his hat. He went to the door of the sitting-room, glanced in, and uttered an exclamation which might have been satisfaction or annoyance.

"Please come in here," rumbled Dr Fell. "All of you, if you will. And close the door."

The usual odor as of damp oilcloth, of old wood and stone, was brought out by the sun in that stuffy room. Angus's photograph, still draped in crepe, faced them from the overmantel. Sun made tawdry the dark, bad daubs of the pictures in their gilt frames, and picked out worn places in the carpet.

"My dear sir," said the lawyer, putting down his hat and brief case on the table which held the Bible. He spoke the words as though he were beginning a letter.

"Sit down, please," said Dr Fell.

A slight frown creased Duncan's high, semi-bald skull.

"In response to your telephone call," he replied, "here I am." He made a humorous gesture. "But may I point out, sir, that I am a busy man? I have been at this house, for one cause or another, nearly every day for the past week. And, grave as the issue has been, since it is now settled —"

"It is not settled," said Dr Fell.

"But – !"

"Sit down, all of you," said Dr Fell.

Blowing a film of ash off his pipe, he settled back, returned the pipe to his mouth, and drew at it. The ash settled down across his waistcoat, but he did not brush it off. He eyed them for a long time, and Alan's uneasiness had grown to something like a breath of fear.

"Gentlemen, and Miss Campbell," continued Dr Fell, drawing a long sniff through his nose. "Yesterday afternoon, if you remember, I spoke of a million-to-one chance. I did not dare to hope for much from it. Still, it had come off in Angus's case and I hoped it might come off in Forbes's. It did."

He paused, and added in the same ordinary tone:

"I now have the instrument with which, in a sense, Alec Forbes was murdered."

The death-like stillness of the room, while tobacco smoke curled up past starched lace curtains in the sunlight, lasted only a few seconds.

"Murdered?" the lawyer exploded.

"Exactly."

"You will pardon me if I suggest that –"

"Sir," interrupted Dr Fell, taking the pipe out of his mouth, "in your heart of hearts you know that Alec Forbes was murdered, just as you know that Angus Campbell committed suicide. Now don't you?"

Duncan took a quick look around him.

"It's quite all right," the doctor assured him. "We four are all alone here – as yet. I have seen to that. You are at liberty to speak freely."

"I have no intention of speaking, either freely or otherwise." Duncan's voice was curt. "Did you bring me all the way out here just to tell me that? Your suggestion is preposterous!"

Dr Fell sighed.

"I wonder whether you will think it is so preposterous," he said, "if I tell you the proposal I mean to make."

"Proposal?"

"Bargain. Deal, if you like."

"There is no question of a bargain, my dear sir. You told me yourself that this is an open-and-shut case, a plain case. The police believe as much. I saw Mr MacIntyre, the Procurator Fiscal, this morning."

"Yes. That is a part of my bargain."

Duncan was almost on the edge of losing his temper.

"Will you kindly tell me, Doctor, what it is you wish of me: if anything? And particularly where you got this wicked and indeed dangerous notion that Alec Forbes was murdered?"

Dr Fell's expression was vacant.

"I got it first," he responded, puffing out his cheeks, "from a piece of blackout material – tar paper on a wooden frame – which should have been up at the window in Forbes's cottage, and yet wasn't.

"The blackout *had been* up at the window during the night, else the lantern-light would have been seen by the Home Guard. And the lantern (if you remember the evidence) *had been* burning. Yet for some reason it was necessary to extinguish the lantern and take down the blackout from the window.

"Why? That was the problem. As was suggested to me at the time, why didn't the murderer simply leave the lantern burning, and leave the blackout in its place, when he made his exit? At first sight it seemed rather a formidable problem.

"The obvious line of attack was to say that the murderer had to take down the blackout in order to make his escape; and, once having made it, he couldn't put the blackout back up again. That is a very suggestive line, if you follow it up. Could he, for instance, somehow have got through a steel-mesh grating, and somehow replace it afterwards?"

Duncan snorted.

"The grating being nailed up on the inside?"

Dr Fell nodded very gravely.

"Yes. Nailed up. So the murderer couldn't very well have done *that*. Could he?"

Duncan got to his feet.

"I am sorry, sir, that I cannot remain to listen to these preposterous notions any longer. Doctor, you shock me. The very idea that Forbes –"

"Don't you want to hear what my proposal is?" suggested Dr Fell. He paused. "It will be much to your advantage." He paused again. "Very much to your advantage."

In the act of taking his hat and briefcase from the little table, Duncan dropped his hands and straightened up. He looked back at Dr Fell. His face was white.

"God in heaven!" he whispered. "You do not suggest – ah – that *I* am the murderer, do you?"

"Oh, no," replied Dr Fell. "Tut, tut! Certainly not."

Alan breathed easier.

It was the same idea which had occurred to him, all the more sinister for the overtones in Dr Fell's voice. Duncan ran a finger round inside his loose collar.

"I am glad," he said, with an attempt at humorous dryness, "I am glad, at least to hear that. Now, come sir! Let's have the cards on the table. What sort of proposition have you which could possibly interest me?"

"One which concerns the welfare of your clients. In short, the Campbell family." Again Dr Fell leisurely blew a film of ash off his pipe. "You see, I am in a position to *prove* that Alec Forbes was murdered."

Duncan dropped hat and briefcase on the table as though they had burned him.

"Prove it? How?"

"Because I have the instrument which was, in a sense, used to murder him."

"But Forbes was hanged with a dressing-gown cord!"

"Mr Duncan, if you will study the best criminological authorities, you will find them agreed on one thing. Nothing is more difficult to determine than the question of whether a man has been hanged, or whether he has first been strangled and then hung up afterwards to simulate hanging. That is what happened to Forbes.

"Forbes was taken from behind and strangled. With what, I don't know. A necktie. Perhaps a scarf. Then those artistic trappings were all arranged by a murderer who knew his business well. If such things are done with care, the result cannot be told from a genuine suicide. This murderer made only one mistake, which was unavoidable. But it was fatal.

"Ask yourself again, with regard to that grated window –"

Duncan stretched out his hands as though in supplication.

"But what is this mysterious 'evidence'? And who is this mysterious 'murderer'?" His eye grew sharp. "You know who it is?"

"Oh, yes," said Dr Fell.

"You are not in a position," said the lawyer, rapping his knuckles on the table, "to prove Angus Campbell committed suicide?"

"No. Yet if Forbes's death is proved to be murder, that surely invalidates the false confession left behind? A confession conveniently written on a typewriter, which could have been written by anybody and was actually written by the murderer. What will the police think then?"

"What are you suggesting to me, exactly?"

"Then you will hear my proposition?"

"I will hear anything," returned the lawyer, going across to a chair and sitting down with his big-knuckled hands clasped together, "if you give me some line of direction. *Who* is this murderer?"

Dr Fell eyed him.

"You have no idea?"

"None, I swear! And I – ah – still retain the right to disbelieve every word you say. *Who* is this murderer?"

"As a matter of fact," replied Dr Fell, "I think the murderer is in the house now, and should be with us at any minute."

Kathryn glanced rather wildly at Alan.

It was very warm in the room. A late fly buzzed against one bright window-pane behind the starched curtains. In the stillness they could distinctly hear the noise of footsteps as someone walked along the hall toward the front.

"That should be our friend," continued Dr Fell in the same unemotional tone. Then he raised his voice and shouted. *"We're in the sitting-room! Come and join us!"*

The footsteps hesitated, turned, and came towards the door of the room.

Duncan got to his feet, spasmodically. His hands were clasped together, and Alan could hear the knuckle-joints crack as he pressed them.

Between the time they first heard the footsteps and the time that the knob turned and the door opened, was perhaps five or six seconds. Alan has since computed it as the longest interval of his life. Every board in the room seemed to have a separate creak and crack; everything seemed alive and aware and insistent like the droning fly against the windowpane.

The door opened, and a certain person came in.

"That's the murderer," said Dr Fell.

He was pointing to Mr Walter Chapman, of the Hercules Insurance Company.

20

Every detail of Chapman's appearance was picked out by the sunlight. The short, broad figure clad in a dark blue suit. The fair hair, the fresh complexion, the curiously pale eyes. One hand held his bowler hat, the other was at his necktie, fingering it. He had moved his head to one side as though dodging.

"I beg your pardon?" he said in a somewhat shrill voice.

"I said, come in, Mr Chapman," answered Dr Fell. "Or should I say, Mr Campbell? Your real name is Campbell, isn't it?"

"What the devil are you talking about? I don't understand you!"

"Two days ago," said Dr Fell, "when I first set eyes on you, you were standing in much the same place as now. I was standing over by that window there (remember?), making an intense study of a full-face photograph of Angus Campbell.

"We had not been introduced. I lifted my eyes from studying the photograph; and I was confronted by such a startling, momentary family likeness that I said to you, '*Which Campbell are you?*'"

Alan remembered it.

In his imagination, the short, broad figure before him became the short, broad figure of Colin or Angus Campbell. The fair hair and washed-out eyes became (got it!) the fair hair and washed-out eyes of that photograph of Robert Campbell in the family album. All these things wavered and changed and were distorted like images in water, yet folded together to form a composite whole in the solid person before them.

"Does he remind you of anyone *now*, Mr Duncan?" inquired Dr Fell.

The lawyer weakly subsided into his chair. Or, rather, his long lean limbs seemed to collapse like a clothes horse as he groped for and found the arms of the chair.

"Rabbie Campbell," he said. It was not an exclamation, or a question, or any form of words associated with emotion; it was the statement of a fact. "You're Rabbie Campbell's son," he said.

"I must insist . . ." the alleged Chapman began, but Dr Fell cut him short.

"The sudden juxtaposition of Angus's photograph and this man's face," pursued the doctor, "brought a suggestion which may have been overlooked by some of you. Let me refresh your memory on another point."

He looked at Alan and Kathryn.

"Elspat told you, I think, that Angus Campbell had an uncanny flair for spotting family resemblances; so that he could tell one of his own branch even if the person 'blacked his face and spoke with a strange tongue.' This same flair is shared, though in less degree, by Elspat herself."

This time Dr Fell looked at Duncan.

"Therefore it seemed to me very curious and interesting that, as you yourself are reported to have said, Mr 'Chapman' always kept out of Elspat's way and would never under any circumstances go near her. It seemed to me worth investigating.

"The Scottish police can't use the resources of Scotland Yard. But I, through my friend, Superintendent Hadley, can. It took only a few hours to discover the truth about Mr Walter Chapman, though the transatlantic telephone call (official) Hadley put through afterwards did not get me a reply until the early hours of this morning."

Taking a scribbled envelope from his pocket, Dr Fell blinked at it, and then adjusted his eyeglasses to stare at Chapman.

"Your real name is Walter Chapman Campbell. You hold, or held, passport number 609348 on the Union of South Africa. Eight years ago you came to England from Port Elizabeth, where your father, Robert Campbell, is still alive: though very ill and infirm. You dropped the Campbell part of your name because your father's name had unpleasant associations with the Hercules Insurance Company, for which you worked.

"Two months ago (as you yourself are reported to have said) you were moved from England to be head of one of the several branches of your firm in Glasgow.

"There, of course, Angus Campbell spotted you."

Walter Chapman moistened his lips.

On his face was printed a fixed, skeptical smile. Yet his eyes moved swiftly to Duncan, as though wondering how the lawyer took this, and back again.

"Don't be absurd," Chapman said.

"You deny these facts, sir?"

"Granting," said the other, whose collar seemed inordinately tight, "granting that for reasons of my own I used only a part of my name, what for God's sake am I supposed to have done?"

He pounced a little, a gesture which reminded the watchers of Colin.

"I could also bear to know, Dr Fell, why you and two Army officers woke me up at my hotel in Dunoon in the middle of last night, merely to ask some tomfool questions about insurance. But let that go. I repeat: what for God's sake am I supposed to have done?"

"You assisted Angus Campbell in planning his suicide," replied Dr Fell; "you attempted the murder of Colin Campbell, and you murdered Alec Forbes."

The color drained out of Chapman's face.

"Absurd."

"You were not acquainted with Alec Forbes?"

"Certainly not."

"You have never been near his cottage by the Falls of Coe?"

"Never."

Dr Fell's eyes closed. "In that case, you won't mind if I tell you what I think you did.

"As you said yourself, Angus came to see you at your office in Glasgow when he took out his final insurance policy. My belief is that he had seen you before. That he taxed you with being his brother's son; that you denied it, but were ultimately compelled to admit it.

"And this, of course, gave Angus the final triple-security for his scheme. Angus left *nothing* to chance. He knew your father for a thorough bad hat; and he was a good enough judge of men to diagnose you as a thorough bad hat too. So, when he took out that final, rather unnecessary policy as an excuse to hang about with you, he explained to you exactly what he meant to do. You would come to investigate a curious death. If there were *any* slip-up, any at all, you could always cover this up and point out that the death was murder because you knew what had really happened.

"There was every inducement for you to help Angus. He could point out to you that you were only helping your own family. That, with himself dead, only a sixty-five-year-old Colin stood between an inheritance of nearly eighteen thousand pounds to your own father; and ultimately, of course, to you. He could appeal to your family loyalty, which was Angus's only blind fetish.

"But it was not a fetish with you, Mr Chapman Campbell. For you suddenly saw how you could play your own game.

"With Angus dead, and Colin dead as well . . ."

Dr Fell paused.

"You see," he added, turning to the others, "the attempted murder of Colin made it fairly certain that our friend here must be the guilty person. Don't you recall that *it was Mr Chapman, and nobody else, who drove Colin to sleep in the tower?*"

Alistair Duncan got to his feet, but sat down again.

The room was hot, and a small bead of sweat appeared on Chapman's forehead.

"Think back, if you will, to two conversations. One took place in the tower room on Monday evening, and has been reported to me. The other took place in this room on Tuesday afternoon, and I was here myself.

"Who was the first person to introduce the word 'supernatural' into this affair? That word which always acts on Colin as a matador's cape acts on a bull? It was Mr Chapman, if you recall. In the tower on Monday evening he deliberately – even irrelevantly – dragged it into the conversation, when nobody had suggested any such thing before.

"Colin swore there was no ghost. So, of course, our ingenious friend had to give him a ghost. I asked before: what was the reason for the mummery of the phantom Highlander with the caved-in face, appearing in the tower room on Monday night? The answer is easy. It was to act as the final, goading spur on Colin Campbell.

"The masquerade wasn't difficult to carry out. This tower here is an isolated part of the house. It has a ground-floor entrance to the outside court, so that an outsider can come and go at will. That entrance is usually open; and, even if it isn't, an ordinary padlock key will do the trick. With the assistance of a plaid, a bonnet, a little wax and paint, the ghost 'appeared' to Jock Fleming. If Jock hadn't been there, anybody else would have done as well."

"And then?"

"Bright and early on Wednesday, Mr Chapman was ready. The ghost story was flying. He came here and (don't you remember?) pushed poor Colin clear over the edge by his remarks on the subject of ghosts.

"What was the remark which made Colin go off the deep end? What was the remark which made Colin say, 'That's torn it,' and swear his oath to sleep in the tower? It was Mr Chapman's shy, sly little series of observations ending, 'This is a funny country and a funny house; and I tell you *I* shouldn't care to spend a night up in that room.'"

In Alan's memory the scene took form again.

Chapman's expression now, too, was much the same as it had been. But now there appeared behind it an edge of desperation.

"It was absolutely necessary," pursued Dr Fell, "to get Colin to sleep in the tower. True, the artificial-ice trick could have been worked anywhere. But it couldn't have been worked anywhere by *Chapman*.

"He couldn't go prowling through this house. The thing had to be done in that isolated tower, with an outside entrance for him to come and go. Just before Colin roared good night and staggered up all those stairs, Chapman could plant the box containing the ice and slip away.

"Let me recapitulate. Up to this time, of course, Chapman couldn't for a second pretend he had any glimmering of knowledge as to how Angus might have died. He had to pretend to be as puzzled as anybody else. He had to keep saying he thought it must be suicide; and rather a neat piece of acting it was.

"Naturally, no mention of artificial ice must creep in *yet*. Not yet. Otherwise the gaff would be blown and he couldn't lure Colin by bogey-threats into sleeping in the tower. So he kept on saying that Angus must deliberately have committed suicide, thrown himself out of the window for no cause at all – as our friend did insist in some detail, over and over – or, if there were any cause, it was something damnable in the line of horrors.

"This was his game *up to the time Colin was disposed of.* Then everything would change.

"Then the apparent truth would come out with a roar. Colin would be found dead of carbon-dioxide poisoning. The artificial ice would be remembered. If it wasn't, our ingenious friend was prepared to remember it himself. Smiting his forehead, he would say that of course this was murder; and of course the insurance must be paid; and where was that fiend Alec Forbes, who had undoubtedly done it all?

"Therefore it was necessary *instantly*, on the same night when Colin had been disposed of, to dispose of Alec Forbes."

Dr Fell's pipe had gone out. He put it in his pocket, hooked his thumbs in the pockets of his waistcoat, and surveyed Chapman with dispassionate appraisal.

Alistair Duncan swallowed once or twice, the Adam's apple moving in his long throat.

"Can you – can you prove all this?" the lawyer asked in a thin voice.

"I don't have to prove it," said Dr Fell, "since I can prove the murder of Forbes. To be hanged by the neck until you are dead, and may God have mercy upon your soul, is just as effective for one murder as for two. Isn't it, Mr Chapman?"

Chapman had backed away.

"I – I may have spoken to Forbes once or twice –" he began, hoarsely and incautiously.

"Spoken to him!" said Dr Fell. "You struck up quite an acquaintance with him, didn't you? You even warned him to keep out of the way. Afterwards it was too late.

"Up to this time your whole scheme had been triple foolproof. For, d'ye see, Angus Campbell really *had* committed suicide. When murder came to be suspected, the one person they couldn't possibly suspect was you; because you weren't guilty. I am willing to bet that for the night of Angus's death you have an alibi which stands and shines before all men.

"But you committed a bad howler when you didn't stay to make sure Colin was really dead after falling from the tower window on Tuesday night. And you made a still worse howler when you climbed into your car afterwards and drove out to the Falls of Coe for your last interview with Alec Forbes. What is the license-number of your car, Mr Chapman?"

Chapman winked both eyes at him, those curious light eyes which were the most disturbing feature of his face.

"Eh?"

"What is the license number of your car? It is" – he consulted the back of the envelope – "MGM 1911, isn't it?"

"I – I don't know. Yes, I suppose it is."

"A car bearing the number MGM 1911 was seen parked by the side of the road opposite Forbes's cottage between the hours of two and three o'clock in the morning. It was seen by a member of the Home Guard who is willing to testify to this. You should have remembered, sir, that these lonely roads are no longer lonely. You should have remembered how they are patrolled late at night."

Alistair Duncan's face was whiter yet.

"And that's the sum of your evidence?" the lawyer demanded.

"Oh, no," said Dr Fell. "That's the least of it."

Wrinkling up his nose, he contemplated a corner of the ceiling.

"We now come to the problem of Forbes's murder," he went on, "and how the murderer managed to leave behind him a room locked up on the inside. Mr Duncan, do you know anything about geometry?"

"Geometry?"

"I hasten to say," explained Dr Fell, "that I know little of what I was once compelled to learn, and wish to know less. It belongs to the limbo of schooldays, along with algebra and economics and other dismal things. Beyond being unable to forget that the square of the hypotenuse is equal to the sum of the square of the other two sides, I have happily been able to rid my mind of this gibberish.

"At the same time it might be of value (for once in its life) if you were to think of Forbes's cottage in its geometrical shape." He took a pencil from his pocket and drew a design in the air with it. "The cottage is a square, twelve feet by twelve feet. Imagine, in the middle of the wall facing you, the door. Imagine, in the middle of the wall to your right, the window.

"I stood in that cottage yesterday; and I racked my brains over that infernal, tantalizing window.

"*Why* had it been necessary to take down the blackout? It could not have been, as I indicated to you some minutes ago, because the murderer had in some way managed to get his corporeal body through the grated window. This, as the geometricians are so fond of saying (rather ill-manneredly, it always seemed to me) was absurd.

"The only other explanation was that the window had to be used in some way. I had examined the steel-wire grating closely, if you remember?" Dr Fell turned to Alan.

"I remember."

"In order to test its solidity, I put my finger through one of the openings in the mesh and shook it. Still no glimmer of intelligence penetrated the thick fog of wool and mist which beclouded me. I remained bogged and sunk until you" – here he turned to Kathryn – "passed on a piece of information which even to a dullard like myself gave a prod and a hint."

"I did?" cried Kathryn.

"Yes. You said the proprietress of the Glencoe Hotel told you Forbes often came out there to fish."

Dr Fell spread out his hands. His thunderous voice was apologetic.

"Of course, all the evidences were there. The hut, so to speak, reeked of fishiness. Forbes's angler's creel was there. His flies were there. His gum boots were there. Yet it was only then, only then, when the fact occurred to me that in all that cottage I had seen no sign of a fishing-*rod*.

"No rod, for instance, such as this."

Impelling himself to his feet with the aid of his stick, Dr Fell reached round to the back of the sofa. He produced a large suitcase, and opened it.

Inside lay, piecemeal, the disjointed sections of a fishing rod, black metal with a nickel-and-cork grip into which were cut the initials, 'A.M.F.' But no line was wound round the reel. Instead, to the metal eyelet on what would have been the end or tip of the joined rod had been fastened tightly with wire a small fishing hook.

"A neat instrument," explained Dr Fell.

"The murderer strangled Forbes, catching him from behind. He then strung Forbes up with those artistic indications of suicide. He turned out the lamp and poured away the remaining oil so that it should seem to have burned itself out. He took down the blackout.

"Then the murderer, carrying this fishing rod, walked out of the hut by the door. He closed the door, leaving the knob of the bolt turned uppermost.

"He went round to the window. Pushing the rod through the mesh of the grating – there was plenty of room for it, since I myself could easily get my forefinger through those meshes – he stretched out the rod in a *diagonal* line, from the window to the door.

"With this hook fastened to the tip of the rod, he caught the knob of the bolt, and pulled toward him. It was a bright, *new* bolt (remember?) so that it would shine by (remember?) the moonlight, and he could easily see it. Thus, with the greatest ease and simplicity, he pulled the bolt toward him and fastened the door."

Dr Fell put the suitcase carefully down on the sofa.

"Of course he had to take the blackout down from the window, and, you see, could not now replace it. Also, it was vitally necessary to take the rod away with him. The handle and reel wouldn't go through the window in any case; and, if he were to pitch the other parts in, his game would be given away to the first spectator who arrived and saw them.

"He then left the premises. He was seen and identified, on getting into his car –"

Chapman let out a strangled cry.

"– by the same Home Guard who had first been curious about that car. On the way back he took the rod apart and threw away its pieces at intervals into the bracken. It seemed too much to hope for a recovery of the rod; but, at the request of Inspector Donaldson, of the Argyllshire County Constabulary, a search was made by the local unit of the Home Guard."

Dr Fell looked at Chapman.

"They're covered with your fingerprints, those pieces," he said, "as you probably remember. When I visited you at your hotel in the middle of the night, with the purpose of getting your prints on a cigarette-case, you were at the same time identified as the man seen driving away from Forbes's cottage just after the time of the murder. Do you know what'll happen to you, my friend? You'll hang."

Walter Chapman Campbell stood with his fingers still twisting his necktie. His expression was like that of a small boy caught in the jam-cupboard.

His fingers moved up, and touched his neck, and he flinched. In that hot room the perspiration was moving down his cheeks after the fashion of side-whiskers.

"You're bluffing," he said, first clearing his throat for a voice that would not be steady. "It's not true, any of it, and you're bluffing!"

"You know I'm not bluffing. Your crime, I admit, was worthy of the son of the cleverest member of this family. With Angus and Colin dead, and Forbes blamed for it, you could go back quietly to Port Elizabeth. Your father is very ill and infirm. He would not last long as heir to nearly eighteen thousand pounds. You could then claim it without ever coming to England or Scotland at all, or being seen by anyone.

"But you won't claim it now, my lad. Do you think you've got a dog's chance of escaping the rope?"

Walter Chapman Campbell's hands went to his face.

"I didn't mean any harm," he said. "My God, I didn't mean any harm!" His voice broke. "You're not going to give me up to the police, are you?"

"No," said Dr Fell calmly. "Not if you sign the document I propose to dictate to you."

The other's hands flew away from his face, and he stared with foggy hope. Alistair Duncan intervened.

"What, sir, is the meaning of this?" he asked harshly.

Dr Fell rapped his open hand on the arm of the sofa.

"The meaning and purpose of this," he returned, "is to let Elspat Campbell live out her years and die happily without the conviction that Angus's soul is burning in hell. The purpose is to provide for Elspat and Colin to the end of their lives as Angus wanted them provided for. That is all.

"You will copy out this document" – Dr Fell took several sheets of paper from his pocket – "or else write, at my dictation, the following confession. You will say that you deliberately murdered Angus Campbell . . ."

"*What?*"

"That you tried to murder Colin, and that you murdered Alec Forbes. That, with the evidence I shall present, will satisfy the insurance companies and the money will be paid. No, I know you didn't kill Angus! But you're going to say you did; and you have every motive for having done so.

"I can't cover you up, even if I wanted to. And I don't want or mean to. But this much I can do. I can withhold that confession from the police for forty-eight hours, in time for you to make a getaway. Ordinarily you would have to get an exit-permit to leave the country. But you're close to Clydeside; and I think you could find an obliging skipper to take you aboard an outgoing ship. If you do that, rest assured that in these evil days they won't bring you back.

"Do that, and I'll give you the leeway. Refuse to do it, and my evidence goes to the police within the next half-hour. What do you say?"

The other stared back.

Terror, befuddlement, and uncertainty merged into suspicious skepticism.

"I don't believe you!" shrilled Chapman. "How do I know you wouldn't take the confession and hand me over to the police straightaway?"

"Because, if I were foolish enough to do that, you could upset the whole apple-cart by telling the truth about Angus's death. You could deprive those two of the money and tell Elspat exactly what her cherished Angus actually did. You could prevent me from achieving the very thing I'm trying to achieve. If you depend on me, remember that I depend on you."

Again Chapman fingered his necktie. Dr Fell took out a large gold watch and consulted it.

"This," Alistair Duncan said out of a dry throat, "is the most completely illegal, fraudulent –"

"That's it," stormed Chapman. "You wouldn't dare let me get away, anyway! It's a trick! If you have that evidence and held up the confession, they'd have you as accessory after the fact!"

"I think not," said Dr Fell politely. "If you consult Mr Duncan there, he will inform you that in Scots law there is no such thing as an accessory after the fact."

Duncan opened his mouth, and shut it again.

"Rest assured," pursued Dr Fell, "that every aspect of my fraudulent villainy has been considered. I further propose that the real truth shall be known to us in this room, and to nobody else. That here and now we swear an oath of secrecy which shall last to the end of our days. Is that acceptable to everyone?"

"It is to me!" cried Kathryn.

"And to me," agreed Alan.

Duncan was standing in the middle of the room, waving his

hands. If, thought Alan, you could imagine any such thing as a sputtering which was not funny, not even ludicrous, but only anguished and almost deathlike, that was his expression.

"I ask you," he said, "I ask you, sir, before it is too late, to stop and consider what you propose! It goes beyond all bounds! Can I, as a reputable professional man, sanction or even listen to this?"

Dr Fell remained unimpressed.

"I hope so," he answered calmly. "Because it is precisely what I mean to carry out. I hope you, of all people, Mr Duncan, won't upset the apple-cart you have pushed for so long and kept steady with such evident pain. Can't you, as a Scotsman, be persuaded to be sensible? Must you learn practicality from an Englishman?"

Duncan moaned in his throat.

"Then," said Dr Fell, "I take it that you have given up these romantic ideas of legal justice, and will row in the same boat with us. The question of life or death now lies entirely with Mr Walter Chapman Campbell. I am not going on with this offer all day, my friend. Well, what do you say? Will you confess to two murders, and get away? Or will you deny both, and hang for one?"

The other shut his eyes, and opened them again.

He looked round the room as though he were seeing it for the first time. He looked out of the windows at the shimmering waters of the loch; at all the domain which was slipping away from him; but at a house cleansed and at peace.

"I'll do it," he said.

The 9:15 train from Glasgow to Euston slid into Euston only four hours late, on a golden sunshiny morning which dimmed even the cavernous grime of the station.

The train settled in and stopped amid a sigh of steam. Doors banged. A porter, thrusting his head into a first-class sleeping compartment, was depressed by the sight of two of the most prim, respectable (and probably low-tipping) stuffed-shirts he had ever beheld.

One was a young lady, stern of mouth and lofty of expression, who wore shell-rimmed spectacles severely. The other was a professional-looking man with an even more lofty expression.

"Porter, ma'am? Porter, sir?"

The young lady broke off to eye him.

"*If* you please," she said. "It will surely be evident to you, *Dr* Campbell, that the Earl of Danby's memorandum, addressed to the French king and endorsed, 'I approve of this; C.R.' by the king himself, can have been inspired by no such patriotic considerations as your unfortunate Tory interpretation suggests."

"This 'ere shotgun don't belong to you, ma'am, does it? Or to you, sir?"

The gentleman eyed him vaguely.

"Er – yes," he said. "We are removing the evidence out of range of the ballistics authorities."

"Sir?"

But the gentleman was not listening.

"If you will cast your mind back, madam, to the speech made by Danby in the Commons in December, 1689, I feel that certain considerations of reason contained therein must penetrate even the cloud of prejudice with which you appear to have surrounded yourself. For example . . ."

Laden with the luggage, the porter trudged dispiritedly along the platform after them. *Floreat scientia!* The wheel had swung round again.